1. **This book may be kept three weeks. It is to be returned on / before the last date stamped below.**
2. **A fine of 20p will be charged for every week or part of week a book is overdue.**

For Ed, Jenny and Caro

Dolores Walshe is author of *Where the Trees Weep*, and has won numerous awards for her plays and poetry. Readings from her work have taken place at the Mandela Concert in Wembley Stadium, and in Dublin, Soweto and Stockholm.

MoonMad

DOLORES WALSHE

WOLFHOUND PRESS

First published by
WOLFHOUND PRESS Ltd
68 Mountjoy Square
Dublin 1

Wolfhound Press receives financial assistance from the Arts Council/An
Chomhairle Ealaíon, Dublin

British Library Cataloguing in Publication Data
Walshe, Dolores
    MoonMad
    I. Title
    823.914 [FS]

    ISBN 0-86327-391-2

This book is fiction. All characters, incidents and names have no connection with
any persons, living or dead. Any apparent resemblance is purely coincidental.

Typesetting: Wolfhound Press
Cover typography: Aileen Caffrey
Cover illustration: Katharine White
Printed by Cox and Wyman Ltd, Reading, Berkshire

Contents

Acknowledgements
'Maeldúin of Africa' was awarded the **Jerusalem Bloomsday Prize** by the James Joyce Cultural Centre, Dublin in 1991. 'The Note' was published in the *Irish Press* New Irish Writing 1987, and was shortlisted for a **Hennessey Award** 1987. 'The Kreeon Rainbow' was published in the *Irish Times* as part of its Summer Library Fiction Series in 1990. 'East of Ireland' appeared in *Wildish Things: An anthology of new Irish women's writing* (Attic Press, 1989).

The Kreeon Rainbow

When Connie answered the phone, she thought it was a crank, the line heavy with mumbled words. 'If you've something to say, say it,' she snapped into the receiver. If she didn't hurry, she'd be late for the badminton lesson. About to hang up, she caught the childish wisp of a voice. 'Please could you send some more kreeons?'

The child obviously had the wrong number, but the 'please' arrested her. Politer than her own children; 'please' was a word Jack and Sally avoided.

'Are you there, Mrs Henderson?' The child's voice panicked.

'Yes, yes, but how do you know my —?'

'I can't make any rainbows.'

Maybe it was a crank after all? As the line continued to mumble, Connie rubbed at a smudge on the hall mirror. When it didn't clear, she finally registered her lipstick, its unevenness a ragged wound slashing her face. So much for the brave new Monday-morning mouth with which she'd planned on storming the world.

'I waited on the kreeons, but they never came.' The small voice was now accusing.

'Kreeons? What are you —?'

'They make lovely rainbows, Sister Agatha says they're special American ones, please can you send some more?'

Sister Agatha. This had to be a kid from the orphanage. Connie lifted a sneakered foot, kicking the sports bag down the hall. It somersaulted, before landing with the soft plop of a dashed hope. She'd never make badminton in time. The instructor'd be miffed, his irritable eye making her nervous as she tried to focus on that bloody shuttlecock. Oh to hell with it, she'd only been going there to kill time! The child's voice was tearful now. 'Johnny Murtagh took my last two. Sister said I mustn't say, because I didn't see him do it, but I just know he did, he's a robber and —!'

'What'd he take?'

'My kreeons from America.'

In the mirror, a woman stared back with dawning eyes. The crayons Jack and Sally's father had sent from the States. She'd retrieved them quietly from the bin in Sally's bedroom, including them in the last parcel she'd sent to the orphanage, a ... month ago, was it?

For a while longer she talked to the child, promising she'd do what she could to get her some more. When she finally hung up, the woman in the mirror was crying. For herself. For her children. For the small scut in the orphanage who'd fixed all her hope on two lousy crayons.

Connie dragged into the kitchen to make tea. The door of the microwave threw back her image clearly as a television screen: a middle-aged woman with blotchy skin and bitter eyes. Hope. There hadn't even been two crayons-worth of it around here lately. Although she hadn't told them out straight, Jack and Sally knew their father wasn't coming back. Yes, their father, she'd be damned if she'd ever again refer to him as her husband, not after the way he'd walked out, his mind cold and indifferent to her as a locked door. God, what she wouldn't give for him to see the children every week his letter landed on the hall floor, its stars and stripes branded on their tight silent faces as they read.

And now Dick wanted his children to visit. 'I'm missing them,' he had written. When she'd read those words this morning, she'd begun to laugh, the sound teetering in the empty house. Thank goodness the children hadn't been here. She stared around the neat kitchen. Perhaps there was still something that needed to be cleaned? But everything gleamed, smirking at her with the idiot smugness of a Stepford housewife in a television commercial, the one who cleaned the house and still had time for tennis, not to mention the magic of a cordon bleu dinner on the table when her Action Man came home, dark, handsome face wreathed in appreciative smiles as he gave his Barbie-doll a designer peck on the lips. How was your day, dear? Oh, wonderful! — I murdered another few million germs lurking in the bathroom. Connie grimaced and lit a cigarette. She hadn't planned it, but somehow she'd become the perfect housekeeper since Dick had left, as if she had to prove something, though what, and to whom, she wasn't sure. She was sure of nothing anymore, save the dull certainty of knowing if you scrubbed a muddy floor, it shone. Cause and effect, simple to grasp. On the table before her, a layer of scum was forming on the untouched mug of tea, as though the liquid needed a skin to shelter under. Just as she sheltered in a mindless round of dusting, cleaning, polishing, where memories kept cropping like errant germs which she swiftly annihilated.

She was still sitting, the tea long gone cold, when the children came in the back door, dropping their schoolbags. 'Pick them up,' she spoke automatically. Instead, they stood looking at her. Six months ago, they'd have hurtled in, a bickering, giggling mix of energies demanding undivided attention as they launched into the trials of the school day. She felt a sudden ache. If only they could be that way again!

'What'd he say in the letter? — Dad.' Jack brought out the last word as though it were a vile taste. Getting the milk and biscuits, Connie kept her face hidden. Normally it was the children he wrote to, the only envelopes addressed to her containing the monthly support cheque. But the cheque wasn't due and they knew it.

'Well?' said Jack, sounding just like his father, eyes grey slits of suspicion behind his glasses.

'He'd like to ... see you.' Connie saw the summer stretching ahead of her, childless. She tried to keep her voice even. 'He wants you to go over for six weeks in the summer.'

'No way!' Jack ran from the kitchen, his biscuits untouched.

Sally was trying not to cry as she ran after him. Connie sat, a vague sense of guilt clouding her satisfaction. Though Dick had asked to see them, not demanded it, she'd deliberately rephrased his request to ensure they'd reject it, wanting the small spiteful triumph of that. What was she becoming? She bit her lip, tasting a sudden rush of salt.

When she went upstairs, Sally was lying on her bed, sucking her thumb again. In Jack's room, the computer was going mad as he punched the keyboard.

'Cut it out!' She raised her voice above the querulous bleeping. Jack ignored her. Bending down, she pulled the plug, plunging the room into silence. Jack stared at her, his face a beef tomato. 'I'm not going!'

'We'll have to ... see.'

'You can't make me!'

'He's your father —'

'I have no father, he's dead!'

'Don't say that!' Connie leaned against the wall, wishing she could go someplace quiet, suck her own thumb. 'He said he'd take you to Disneyland —'

'That kip! I don't want to go!'

'Neither do I.' It was Sally, trembling in the open door. Connie turned. 'But Mickey Mouse is your favourite —'

'Not any more.' The small voice sounded punished. 'It's ... it's kid's stuff ... isn't it?' Sally looked at her brother, her eyes pleading. But Jack stayed tight-lipped. Connie dug her nails into her palms. Twelve years old, and already a cold pinched wisdom in his face. What had Dick done, just what the hell had he done, goddamn him!

'All right,' she said finally. 'I'll talk to you about it later.' But they both knew she wouldn't. She hadn't been able to talk to them at all about their father.

'Do either of you have any of those crayons he sent, you know, the fancy ones that make rainbows when you swirl them?'

Jack looked at Sally. 'No,' he said. 'Right Sal?' Sally nodded, putting her thumb back in her mouth. Connie knew he was lying. She told them about the phone call. In the pause, the muted shrieks of children sounded in the street. Jack hadn't been out to play since he realised Dick had left for good. He was afraid of questions he didn't know how to answer. Afraid of the neighbours' pity. The same reason she'd been avoiding people.

When Jack finally spoke, his face was sheepish. 'I'll have a look,' he said. 'Think I saw one somewhere.'

'Thanks.' Connie pushed a streal of hair out of Sally's eyes. 'I'll phone Sister Agatha, maybe we could take it over on Saturday, do us good to get out —'

'I don't want to!'

Connie moved out onto the landing, forcing herself to sound cheerful. 'We'll all go, ages since we did something together ... as a ... family.' The word sounded hollow.

Jack scowled at the old sycamore framed in the window.

Looking at him, Sally took her thumb out. 'Don't want to.' Back went the thumb, corking her mouth.

'You'll do as you're told, the pair of you! We're going to the orphanage, and we're going to, to, have a good time —!' She stopped. A ridiculous thing to say. Jack obviously thought so too, peering at her in a combination of owlish astonishment and dismissal over his glasses. The spit of his father. And, come to think of it, his father's father, who had never liked her much to begin with: who had, in fact, gone to his grave hugging his dislike close to his chest, a singular man for sticking to his guns. Connie shivered. As though both men were present in the room, and all the men who had preceded them, resurrect, the gulf of distance, the march of centuries wiped out in an instant by the casual arrogance of her son's inherited glance. Goddamn it, did he have to look at her like that? She stamped her foot, the sound swallowed in the carpet. 'You're coming, like it or lump it!'

'Yeh, we always have to do what you want, even Dad had to, maybe that's why he went away!' Jack stepped back, as though he were afraid she'd run at him.

It took Connie a few moments to get the words out. 'How ... dare you speak to your mother like —!'

'You always made Daddy pick his clothes up off the floor.' Sally, pointing a wet, shrivelled thumb.

Connie fought an inane urge to squeal. 'Of course I did —! D'you think I should've picked up —?' She caught her breath, seeing it. Dick had left, that was all they knew. She hadn't known how to tell them about their new half-sister. She still didn't know how to face it herself. Turning away, she hurried downstairs, a cold hand closing on something raw and tender inside, its grip vice-like. They blamed her. Dick had deserted them but, somehow, she was responsible. Her eyes stung. They couldn't blame Dick because it'd mean doubting him. And if they didn't blame her, they'd have to blame themselves. Christ. She'd have to find the courage to talk to them. Dredge it from the swamp of her own misery.

———

In the end, they came with her, the thumb dropping from Sally's mouth as she stared upwards at the old granite walls. 'It's a castle,' she whispered.

'It's a dump,' said Jack.

Sally remembered herself. 'A ... a dump,' she echoed. Connie sighed as she climbed from the car.

Sister Agatha was all bustle, the crayon swiped from Connie's hand before she could protest.

'Art class's just beginning, Miss O'Brien's a stickler, she does it for free, you see,' said Sister Agatha, handing the crayon to a small boy. 'Give it to Mary Donegan, hurry now!'

Connie was disappointed. She'd wanted the pleasure of seeing the child's face.

Sister Agatha showed them around, thanking Connie for the old toys and comics she sent regularly. Connie waved her aside. 'We have enough, too much, in fact,' she said, embarrassed at Jack's mutinous gaze.

They went into the art room as class ended. A little blonde cherub looked up, smiling. It had to be her.

Sister Agatha broke off greeting the wizened teacher to roar at the sea of faces. 'Mary Donegan, come and thank Mrs Henderson!'

Connie looked at the cherub. Instead, a skinny stick in a dull frock rose from her place, shuffling to stand before her. Connie forced a smile, taking the picture the child proffered, a rainbow sitting on a woman's head, all frizzed, as though it'd just had a perm. In the trough of every wave, a sun was rising.

'Why, it's magic!' said Connie. The child's face peeped at her through lifeless flaps of hair. 'I can do better ones.' The thin mouth grinned.

'Can you, now? Well, how about you coming home with us for lunch? Then maybe you can show me?' She smiled down, wishing she'd kept quiet. Jack would be livid.

———

Mary Donegan sat in the middle in the back as Connie drove slowly, watching them in the rear-view mirror. Sally's thumb was dithering about her chest. 'Could I plait your hair?'

Mary nodded. 'Yeh, but it won't stay, it's too slippery. Everyone says it's mousey, but I don't mind, I like mice.'

'Y'know what we call you?' Jack made a face. 'The Kreeon Rainbow.'

Connie wanted to throttle him. 'Stop it!'

Mary turned to him. 'And you're Growler, you don't speak to people, you growl.' There was a small silence.

'Or, Orphan Annie, maybe that's what I'll call you, Little —'

'Shut up, Jack!' Connie put her foot on the brake and was hooted from behind.

'I like being an orphan.'

Jack's mouth gaped. She might've said something sacrilegious. Connie pulled over to the side, stopping the car. How dare he, dare he behave —! She swivelled to face him. But he wasn't looking at her. Engrossed in each other, none of them seemed to notice she'd stopped. She opened the window and lit a cigarette. Ahead, through the windscreen, the calm orbs of the pedestrian crossing blinked.

'Is it nicer than having a Mam and Dad of your own?' Sally was saying as Connie glanced in the mirror.

'I don't know.' Mary shrugged. 'But I like the orphanage. I like Sister Agatha and —'

'Maybe not nicer, but maybe it's better,' Jack said suddenly. 'Least if you're an orphan, your parents can't dump you. We're half-orphans anyway.'

Connie held her breath against the pain that knifed somewhere in the pit of her.

'Is your Dad gone to Heaven?'

Sally spoke through her thumb. 'No, he's gone to America.'

For the first time in months, Connie felt an urge to laugh. But Sally's tone stifled it, the thin childish wail making distance synonymous with the geography of death.

'Sister'd never dump us ...' Mary was saying, '... she'd never —'

'How'd you know?' Jack's voice was rough.

'Because she's a nun.'

Jack digested this, struggled with it, then nodded. Somehow, the answer had to suffice, as though he needed to believe with gilt-edged certainty in some kind of fidelity, even if it had to be that of a nun. Mary was tucking the flaps of hair behind her ears. 'Why'd your Dad go away?'

'Gon't know,' said Sally, inside her thumb.

Jack cleared his throat. 'He didn't ... love us ... I suppose.'

Connie turned. 'That's not true!'

The three of them looked at her, eyes wide.

She struggled to get the words out. 'Your father ... loves you both ... very much. He ... misses you very much. It's just that ...' Turning away to hide it, she stared through the windscreen.

'Does he ... love you?' Jack's voice was nervous. Connie hissed, the question winding her. She wanted to lie, Christ how she wanted to lie, she wanted to put the sun back in the heavens for all of them! 'No,' she said eventually. Opening her hands, she stared at the grooves her nails had made. 'No.'

It had begun, finally. In the small, enclosed space, the silence rang tense with the absence of sound, as if even the children had paused between breaths. She hauled it to the surface of her lips, each word leaden in the stillness as she ejected it: 'No. Your father does not love me anymore.' Ahead, the orange orbs blinked, regardless. They should have shattered, she thought, to a myriad pieces, the earth should have split, the clouds dropped like rocks.

A thin drizzle began to fall, its pins and needlepoints pricking the windscreen with uniform equanimity. Her hand shook as she turned the key in the ignition.

MoonMad

It's the first Saturday of the month and Tommy's eyes are twin suns again, firing up his blue moon face. It's the reason I go along with him, just for the lift it gives me seeing all that pent-up light. Enough to dazzle you it is. And it won't die down into the pit of his stomach 'till we come back around tea-time to the house and the kids.

Ma's minding them again today. She's good that way, though she thinks Tommy's crazy, moon-mad she calls him. I wish she wouldn't call him that, after all, he's a good husband to me, better than the Da any day, though that wouldn't be hard, the aul shite's drinking again, I can tell by the way she keeps picking on Tommy. I'm sorry now I ever told her what it is we do on every first Saturday.

So what, so Tommy gets fed up being stuck in the house all the time since the building in Black Alley was condemned and he had to close the chipper down; all right, so he gets a bit hyper like, on and off. Then again, who wouldn't?

Ma doesn't understand. Though she was all smiles at first, when it was only a new chip shop Tommy began searching for. It was later, when he began bussing it over to the library in Tranquillity Grove for a read of the big newspapers, that she couldn't stomach it. Getting above his station, she called it. I said I'd like to know what our station is, exactly what it is, that if she ever found out, I hoped she'd be good enough to tell us; we could all do with knowing.

Every Thursday Tommy goes. And it isn't the news in the papers he's bothered with. It's the 'Property' sections. Well, if I'm honest, I should say it straight off. He sometimes, well, he nicks them. After all, as he says himself, who around there would be interested in the property sections, except maybe for a free gaff to squat in?

Thank God his indigestion is gone this morning. We're to meet the estate agent in Bewleys' Oriental Café, the one in Grafton Street, and that's the nearest I'll ever get to Japan or Ceylon or wherever the tea comes from. Orr-eee-nnn-tall. Like I'm rolling a big glass marble round me mouth, one with lovely green ferns floating inside. No, my. My mouth. Must keep a watch on that.

I just hope it all goes right, that's my prayer. Sweet Jesus if you really are up there, you'd better be listening after all I've gone and offered up to you lately! And suffered.

I'll say this for Tommy, he always plans it perfectly, the whole day always goes like clockwork. So far, every single estate agent has believed us, though I leave most of the talking to Tommy, he sounds much better than me when we're putting on airs.

And it's him who decides what we'll wear each time, not but that he always wears the same outfit himself: stiff white shirt with the black suit, his funeral suit, God I hate it, but it's the only one he's got. And his orange tie, for a bit of flash, he says. As if it was his idea. I say nothing, just smile away, glad it's forcing my mind off the suit.

I have to wear my navy skirt with the good blouse. My black high-heels of course. There's a snag in the knee of my tights, but I'm hoping to God it'll hold. Two for the price of one in the Jobber's Mart, serves me right for thinking I was getting a bargain. I've twisted the snag in sideways so Tommy can't spot it. It's the only thing that makes him nervous, feeling we aren't perfect.

Sometimes when I'm dolled up like this, I get a shock when I look in the mirror. It's like someone's put a stamp on me to say I'm the real thing, official like, even though right then I'm playing at being someone else. I get so impressed I stare for ages till it comes over me, this feeling, strange, that if I was to walk away from Tommy when we get into town, that, well, some other man would come up to me, a very smart man with a pin-striped suit and a gold watch chained to his chest. He'd take me home to this mansion of a place steeped to the gills in shaggy carpets, and he'd hand me a glass of sparkling drink, champagne maybe, then he'd smile and say I was his long-lost wife, that this was where I belonged. Stupid.

And if you want to know, the worst bit of all is I'd believe him. I'd believe him and I'd just stay there. I don't know what gets into me imagining a thing like that. Thicko Ma. That's what Natashya would say. If she was alive. Yes my heart. My truly and only and ever first-born. Though she'd be smiling to take the sting out of it. My Natashya.

But that's not the half of the way I am. I'm always pretending. Even when I'm not dressed up, when I'm wearing my real clothes. I pretend to the Jobber that I'm broke out the door when I've won a fiver on the Pools, just to get him to knock his price down, and I pretend to Ma that I'm not in the least bit worried about Tommy. She swallows it no bother, though sometimes I wonder if she just pretends because it saves her from having to worry alongside of me. I often wonder what she's like on the inside of her skin, what she's really like. Maybe there's no such a thing as the real her or the real anybody except new-born babies who don't know how to pretend like the rest of us. Who knows?

I don't do any imagining this morning, I haven't got the energy. Attracta had me up half the night with the new back teeth swelling her gums to bursting. In the end I gave in and let her into the bed between us. The little whore snuggled into the dip and fell asleep quicker than you could blink. I could've shot her. Then Tommy stretched across and started feeling me and I could've shot him. I don't know what got into him with the baby snuffling away in the middle. It gave me a right shock the way his hand came sudden out of the dark. I got another one this morning when I touched the metal jumping down off the bus. My body's definitely getting more electric as I get older, which is a howl as well as a mystery, weird, I wonder why it is?

When I couldn't get back to sleep last night I just lay there pressing my eyeballs like I did when I was a brat, so the dark would spark and make some stars. But my eyes pained, so I stopped. I lay there, the jizz gone out of me, too tired even to turn Tommy out of his snores. Maybe that's what happened God too, maybe He started out with great intentions but when things kept going wrong

He got tired trying to put them right, real deep down dog bone tired deep down inside and so He just withered up and stopped. Or maybe He blew Himself up. Sometimes lately, when I'm standing in the scullery with the telly going in the front room and Tommy sitting staring but not seeing it and not even hearing the screeches of the kids well I feel like I'm going to blow up myself.

When I told Ma what they were saying on telly about God being the Big Bang, she said she didn't want to hear, it was blasphemy, that I ought to be ashamed. I was all ready to argue the toss. But when I saw her scrunched face I shut up. What right have I to make her afraid? She has a hard enough life as it is with the Da. Still, it's a pity. She may have got married young like me, but she's never moved with the times.

Tommy and me don't have tea in Bewleys or anything. The two of us just stroll out of the Men's and Ladies' a couple of minutes after it's time to meet your man the estate agent inside the front door. A Mr Holmes it is this time, an aul dandy of a man from one of the big places on Dawson Street. Tommy cracks a joke about the name Holmes hitting the nail right on the head, seeing as it's exactly what we're searching for. Aul Mr Holmes doubles up laughing so hard I can tell he's tired to death hearing this one, but Tommy's smile is coming out his ears. We all stroll out together, just as if we'd come from our breakfast at one of the lovely pink marble table-tops.

When we're on our way in Mr Holmes' car, Tommy takes care to ask if we can be dropped back afterwards to the underground car park in Abbey Street. This is just to fool Mr Holmes. In actual fact it's near our bus terminus.

I don't think we're being dishonest, not really. Everybody has a right to look at a nice house that's for sale, even if they don't stand a snowman's chance in Mexico of ever buying it. That's what Ma says. She mixes up sayings just to get on my wick.

Mr Holmes' car is plush. Tommy's in the front talking ninety to the dozen. He sounds like he's eaten the property section of every newspaper going. This is the part I like best. No one's watching and

I can relax. There's lovely waltzing music behind my head. I could listen to it forever.

I always make sure to sit well out of sight after that time I found your man from Brookfield Properties watching me real hard in the rear-view mirror. It set my heart racing something fierce, thinking he was getting suspicious, but it all worked out grand that day too. Nowadays I don't get too nervous anymore. You can get used to anything. And Tommy's very careful. So far we've never been back to the same estate agent twice.

When we get out of the city and zip past our council estate, I can't help grinning. If the neighbours could see us. But even the kids don't know, when they ask where we go, we always just say it's our day off. Which makes Ma roll her eyes to Heaven.

You can't say we're conning anybody, not when no money changes hands. Just we're wasting people's time I suppose. To-day's house is in Wicklow, I wish Tommy hadn't picked one so far out, it's an awful drive for Mr Holmes. Coolavaun House, it's called.

It's stuffy in the car with the sunshine. Not to mention Tommy's spoofing, his words falling over themselves, filling up the spaces in the air. Making me even hotter.

Nothing's moving in the fields. The cows are crowded under the trees, shagged with the heat. The sheep aren't real at all, nailed up flat on the hills exactly as if the kids had drawn them. Sometimes lately, when they draw me and colour me in, always the same lumpy shape with a big lipsticky smile plastered to my face, well, I wish they wouldn't. I look at myself pinned down flat on their pages and even though my mouth is open as if it was smiling, I can't see that at all. Instead what I see it's open for is to scream. A huge red scream, the kind you know if you started you'd never be able to stop. But nobody else seems to notice, not even that nice new teacher who sticks little gold stars on their drawings every week.

Now and again I have to close the window, the smell of manure would shrivel your imagination. Even with my eyes closed I can tell when we rush past gaps in the ditch the way the air sounds.

Like the Da when he's had a skinful and he snarls his way into our place looking for Ma.

I only get suspicious when we turn into the mangled drive leading up to the house. You'd swear you were on the inside of a stone-crusher the way the tyres are grinding. The sky's shut out by the trees, like we're driving up the aisle of a cool green cathedral with the sun bursting the leaves turning them to bits of coloured glass.

Even Tommy shuts up. All of a sudden I feel sad. I don't know why. The more I stare at how deep the colour is all round us the sadder I get. Nobody speaks. Everything is strange for a second, weird, like we're pressed on the inside of some miracle, the shadows of the branches dancing and flitting and swirling all round us, hurrying and pushing us on, squeezing us close and tight together so it's hard to tell which one of us in the car is which. But when Mr Holmes speaks, his voice is like a fist out of nowhere and we all snap apart.

What he says stomachs me. One hundred and twenty-eight rooms, that's what he says, and a cucumber isn't in it for the coolness of those words. I stare hard at the mole bobbing on the back of Tommy's neck, hoping he'll say there must be some mistake, hoping it isn't true. But the mole just keeps on bobbing.

'Then that'd be about two thousand pounds a room so?' Tommy says. And that's when I see what Ma must've seen all along, that Tommy is playing this for real. Suddenly I'm clammy in my skin, there's no air in the car but I'm shaking so much it takes me ages to roll down the window. Maybe thirty thousand pounds, maybe even forty, but there's no way Mr Holmes can be eejit enough to believe we could afford a house that costs, God I can't even bear to multiply the numbers. Just wait 'till I get Tommy home, I'll reef him.

Even knowing now what I'm in for doesn't help when we round the bend and see it there staring down at us with a string of brassy suns in the windows that'd blind you for a week. Any minute now the sky'll darken and lightening will split it. Then that big drunk door'll whinge open and Dracula will stagger out to lean against one of the cracked pillars, looking just as much at home standing on those stone steps as Our Lady grinning in a grotto. Moon-bloody-mad, oh Ma was right!

I don't know how I get through the next hour, it's like I'm looking at it all through the fog we get over our estate in winter because everybody's burning the Jobber's cheap coal, though we all know we're not supposed to.

But even with the jitters, what I manage to take in of the house strikes me as no great shakes. There's no air in the place, and the smell of rot in some of the rooms would make you want to run outside to bury your face in the big stretches of grass. Even Tommy looks none too happy with any of it.

When Mr Holmes excuses himself and taps off to one of the mouldy bathrooms, I'm all set to tackle Tommy. But as soon as I open my mouth, he asks me for an indigestion sweet, he's been chewing buckets of them all week. He's flushed and sweating with the heat, so I say nothing, just hand him the sweet from my bag. Seems to me he's suffering enough right now.

We just go on standing there in the ballroom, waiting for Mr Holmes. It's gi-normous, the room. The sun's coming in all the windows together, so you'd think you were walking on pools of hot gold instead of a wooden floor. There's all these pink plaster angels and fruit and flowers on the ceiling, and women with no clothes on. Goddesses, Mr Holmes said they were. And nymphs.

'Nymphos, more like,' Tommy whispered with a grin that big I nearly died. Thank God Mr Holmes didn't catch it.

You'd get dizzy looking up at them. But they make you feel a bit wild somehow, like when you want to dance. I'm sorry now I'm not wearing my aul loose skirt. The music from Mr Holmes' car is still playing away in my head. I know it's daft, but I kick off my shoes for the hell of it and twirl round a bit. Then there's this crash behind me. When I open my eyes, Tommy's lying on the floor. Out cold, his face the colour of a turnip and his breathing all locked in his chest.

The next minute I'm out in the open running across the big stretch of grass that leads to the fields and for some reason I'm in my bare feet. There's a gap in the bushes and I squeeze through into a meadow with piles of humming poppies splashed about like paint. Beautiful. Like stepping into a birth. My Natashya. The love that was you in my womb, your crying all gummed with petals of blood till the nurse cleaned your mouth and then the sweet bawls of you nearly deafening me.

But maybe you weren't crying after all, maybe what you were doing was screaming. Even then. Maybe even before then, as far back as when I thought you were kicking like a butterfly to life inside me.

I can hear Mr Holmes calling out somewhere away in the distance. I know I should go back, but I can't. Instead I'm dancing, deep into the field, the grass tickling far up under my skirt. Deeper and deeper in I go till I'm so giddy from twirling that I can't hear Mr Holmes anymore.

Suddenly everything's reeling and I fall down. All round me the grass is tinkling, like I've smashed it. The sky's the blue of the Blessed Virgin's cloak, and it's spinning fast, like it can't wait for the world to drag itself into tomorrow. Well, I'm on the side of the world, I whisper, though I don't know what I mean, but I pat the ground real gentle because I can feel Natashya laying in it.

I stay this way for ages but the sky still keeps on running. No matter how fast it runs I can imagine the pictures even faster, how it's taking Mr Holmes and me ages to get him out to the car what with all the weight he's put on, me holding him the best I can, sort of twisted across the back seat with his head in my lap while Mr Holmes drives, the branches flitting and dancing all round us again but like they're lashing out at us now trying to hold us back and the green so deep it'd kill your eyes.

And how I don't know I'm crying 'till Mr Holmes reaches over his shoulder with the hanky floating in his hand and me wanting to blurt it all out right then about Natashya about the chip shop closing about everything. But when I look at Mr Holmes in the driver's mirror, I know he knows already. And somehow I know too that he doesn't mind us wasting his time. It's all there in the way he keeps his nice brown eyes glued to the road.

I'm afraid to see how Tommy looks in the pictures so instead I pretend I can see the snag in the knee of my tights, still holding, but only just. I stare real hard at it before I close my eyes to say the words: sweet Jesus, if you're up there, make it hold 'till next month, 'till our next first Saturday, so Tommy can take me out again, moon-mad as ever, the two small suns still there, still firing up his eyes. I whisper the words over and over till the sky slows down.

I just missed this pile of poppies when I fell. The breeze is blowing them over my eyes, splashing their hard little clots on the sky. Like the morning she slipped from between my legs, daubs of my blood drying on her lovely skin.

You can get some kind of drug from poppies, but it wasn't the kind she was doing when she died.

Still, there must have been poppies then too, though I couldn't see them, loads of them, a whole field of them, moving quickly so quickly all through her insides.

The Caller

He stood looking out, his wide trunk blocking the trickle of light from the window.

'D'you think she'll really do it?' I watched his back, the blunt edge of his shoulders, and tried to feel some relief in his lack of tension.

'Hard to say. A grey Monday morning. Raining. It don't exactly help.' He swivelled, a small, hard bullet, his narrowed gaze tracking my face, making me uneasy. I stared past him into the spilling window. Californian rain.

'It's pissing.' I fiddled with my earrings, looking down at the words I'd crammed on the report sheet.

'How'd you rate her?'

'Ten.' I'd have given her eleven, but the lethality scale for potential suicides didn't run that high.

'Taking into account the effect she's had on you, I'd say she's closer to an eight.'

For the first time since he'd arrived, I drew a decent breath. 'But she said she was going to drive her car off the highway. That was the last thing she said. I've never been hung up on before.'

'First is the worst.' He grinned.

'You're a great help, Rolf, you know that?'

'You Irish are born worriers. You want a de-caff?' He moved towards the coffee machine thrumming in the corner.

'No, the ordinary stuff.' Searching for the stapler, I lit on the clock. Harry would kill me. 'Forget the coffee. I haven't time.'

The private line erupted as though he'd heard me: Harry, his words spitting in my ear. 'What're you playing at? You shouldda been here by now. Get the hell back quick as you can.' He hung up.

'Harry?' Rolf stood, eyes like windows, drinking it in. 'You okay? You two had a row or something?' He held out a plastic cup. He never stopped raking.

'I told him I'd be home by seven, that's all.'

'What gives with — ?'

'I'm a counsellor, not a caller.' I said it as lightly as I could. 'Phone me if there's any news, will you?' I didn't wait for his answer but it chased me down the stairs.

'Get some sleep.'

Fat chance. The children had a day off. The most I could expect was to stretch out while they watched television.

Driving on the highway was like skating blindfolded. In the deluge, the speeding cars kept up a barrage of spray. I limped uneasily into the outside lane and a horn blasted. I hooted back, cursing at the truck that overtook me with a brown arm shoved out, middle finger rigidly poking the sky.

I could smell his temper at the front door. He was pacing furiously, the room diminished by his dark bulk. I moved in to stand by the wall.

'Look, I'm really sorry, Harry. There was this emergency. The call came in just before I finished shift. Once you answer it you can't hand over to anybody else. I even had to get Rolf in.'

He spat something as he grabbed his briefcase and tore into the hall.

I followed. 'I should've let one of the other volunteers take it. Don't worry, I'll know better next time.'

He turned, 'Next time? There won't be a frigging next time. Y'wanna do charity work, why can't you be like any normal wife 'n do it in the day-time?'

'I'm not your bloody wife! We live together, that's all.' I was sorry as soon as I said it.

'Yeah, I'm beginning to see the difference.' The screen door crashed after him.

'Will you be late?' I tried to salvage something.

But he ignored me as he plunged in the downpour to the car. I slammed the door and thumped back in to dial the Centre.

'Rolf? I forgot to mention it in the report. She said she worked for a veterinary clinic locally. That she'd access to drugs if she wanted to —'

'Go to bed, Emma. It's all here.'

I listened guiltily to the tiredness in his voice. I knew from some of the other counsellors he'd already lost two nights this week.

'Ring me if —'

'Get some sleep.' He hung up.

Frustrated, I went to call the children. Three hang-ups in less than two hours. Great. I shook the coarse muesli into the bowls, the dust rising like steam. Harry's latest breakfast fad. Fibre, the coarser the better. I didn't mind. Since he'd moved in, the children were eating much better. And he'd taken over the mortgage. I was able to give up work. Money became something to spend. That bloody woman. Jesus, if she meant it.

I took my coffee to the kitchen window but in the rippling glass I could only see the blur of the pear trees. Turn on the radio and listen for news? No. Every report would set my heart jigging. Better to sweat it. No news is no news. I set my cup clattering on the draining-board, hands shaking from lack of sleep.

'Mom! Remote's doing it again. He won't let me watch Romper Room!' Eve's high-pitched shriek sent me running to the living room.

'Stoppit right now. Tom, let go of her.' But I was too tired to summon any real spirit.

'No way. Not until she stops calling me that.'

'Remote! Remote! You'll turn into a robot. Ow, that hurt. You're real mean. Mommmmy!'

And it was only eight-thirty. If Rolf would ring. Just tell me they'd located her. Alive and kicking. Screaming even. I didn't care. As long as she was breathing.

Damn her panting breath, her tears, her thin, hopeless voice oozing its way into my ear.

My eyes stung. I lay on the couch, the children finally sprawled before the television. The morning inched by, the rain a flock of swallows against the wooden roof. As I dozed, the pump started up, forcing out the water collecting under the house. When it came, I picked it up before the end of the first ring.

'Rolf?'

'Don't wait dinner.' He hung up before I could speak. Cursing him, I dragged to the kitchen to get the children's lunch. It was mid-afternoon before Rolf called.

'No sweat. She's fine. Name's Alice, by the way, not the "Ann" she gave you.'

'How'd you find her?'

'Stroke of luck. An outreach call from her landlady. Woman was worried. It fitted when she mentioned Alice'd once worked for a vet, though that was more'n a year ago.'

Her landlady. I thought of the lies she'd told me about living with him. The hatred in the house. She'd tricked me. Cheated. Filled me with it. All for nothing. I felt sick. I didn't realise I was ranting till he cut in on me.

'She wasn't kidding. All that suffering was for real. She moved out two years ago. It's only coming to a head now, poor kid.'

'Poor kid! What about me?' I winced, wishing I'd kept my mouth shut.

'What about you?' His tone level, ever the psychiatrist. I shut up.

'Listen. Nobody owes you anything in this business. You decided to become a counsellor, remember? I warned you when you took the course how tough it'd be. Theory's no sweat. It's the practical's the real test. Three volunteers have opted out already. Now, can you handle it or no? Emma? You still there?'

'Yes.'

'You hear me?'

'I heard.'

'You wanna talk? I'm real busy right now but I could drop by later.'

'No. Harry's working late.'

'What's that got to do with it? It wasn't a proposition.'

I knew that. I was about the only woman in the Centre he'd shown no interest in. Much to my relief.

'I simply meant I have the children to cope with. And I haven't slept all day. I want to get to bed myself.'

'One's thing bugging me. Why'd you switch to the nights? I thought the mornings suited you with the kids at school? If I were Harry I'd —'

'Where is she now?'

'Who?'

'Alice.'

'On her way to the County Clinic. She's agreed to see a therapist.'

'Psychiatric?'

'Probably. But the therapist'll decide.'

'Then she's out of my hair. I don't have to worry —'

'Maybe. First time callers stand the best chance. You're in, lemme see, Wednesday? I'll fill you in then. And Emma? Nicely done.'

When I hung up it dawned on me. He'd been talking about the way I fobbed him off. He could go hang. I'd slit my throat before I'd tell him.

I was off the hook. She was alive. But I couldn't shake her, her words hammering like the rain on the roof. I stared at the sodden swamp in the garden. In a couple of days, there would be a thin wash of green underlying the yellow stubble that covered the low hills behind. Almost like home.

Only when the children were tucked up, did I manage to shut her out, Harry's lateness beginning to niggle. I couldn't sleep when he wasn't here. Reaching under the bed, I dragged out Jack's old baseball bat and leaned it against the nightstand. Jack. I didn't want to look. I had looked too often lately. But her voice started up with the others, urging. I took the picture from the drawer. When I'd snapped it, Eve was still in me. But he was holding Tom. Tightly. Tightly. The sickness already in the stretch of his skin, pulling me back to it. I closed my eyes and repeated the words: Jack is a nothing now. A nothing except the frown on Eve's face and the shrill in Tom's laugh. That is all I have to remember.

It was late. Maybe Harry would stay at the apartment? Sitting in bed, I flicked through the channels on the remote control. News on several. Litanies of crime. Then the westerns, soap operas, old black and whites; the cops and robbers finally taking me through to Doctor Prince. I blinked and tried to concentrate but my mind hadn't caught up with the speed of my eye. I flicked back. There. A child emptying a bottle of brightly coloured pills. Stuffing them, stuffing them in. Some dropping to the counter to clatter in a contrived echo as the camera zooms in on one twitching like a top out of orbit. I careered through the channels to Doctor Prince and blinked again to blot out the kaleidoscope.

How could Tom keep doing it? At it for months now, endlessly zooming through the channels, watching nothing and everything. Driving Eve crazy. Maybe I should ask Rolf. No. I listened to Doctor Prince as he stared into my bedroom.

'... to find the answers. You wanna know if you'll be welcome in His house? Then ask yourself, brother, and you too, sister, what have you done lately for Jesus? Ain't no use going to visit Jesus in His house if you ignore him in the street ...'

I lay back on the pillows and closed my eyes, locking out her ugliness as I homed into the voice.

'You watching this crap again?'

I hadn't heard him come in. He switched off the set.

'You sleeping?' He knew I wasn't.

'I thought you might have stayed at the flat.'

'If I was going to, I'd a called.' He slung his jacket on the end of the bed. I watched him walk to the drawers and thrust his hand into the bowl of chestnuts. He picked up the nutcracker and came to sit next to me.

'Want some?'

I didn't. I'd spent ten minutes brushing off layers of velvet. But I watched the blue vice of his jaw tighten and nodded, hoping to avert it. He liked me to show I believed in his crazes.

He cracked one open, peeling the inner skin to reveal the creamy ivory of the nut.

'I nearly did. Stay in town.' The nut lay in his hand, about as big as a peanut in the paw of an ape. 'Thought maybe it'd be worth having a last crack at it.' He grinned, holding up the nutcracker. I didn't say anything.

'Hey, come on.'

I couldn't bear it. I turned as he reached, pulling the cover over my head. Immediately he yanked it back, dragging me round to face him.

'You talked to Rolf today?'

'Yes.'

'You told him you're gonna give up nights?'

'No, I haven't.'

He let go and walked to the end of the bed. For a moment he stood there, his back to me. Then he turned. 'When're you gonna tell him?'

'I'm not.'

'Not?'

'I'm not going to tell him because I'm not giving up the nights.' I said it as slowly and evenly as I could.

'You know what you're doing?'

'I know.'

'No you don't. You don't have a clue.' He slammed his fists against the brass rails and the bed shook. 'What I'm saying is, you're on your own. You and your baseball bat and that evangelist freak. I'm out.' He leaned heavily on the rail. 'On your own, kid. Got that?'

I pulled the quilt up to my neck to hide the way I was shaking. 'I hear you.'

'Hearing's one thing. I hope you understand what it means.'

'Just go, will you?' It sounded good. Confident.

I saw the hate cut in his eyes. The glitter of it. 'Christ, you're a first-class bitch.' He moved suddenly.

'Don't touch me!'

He stood still, his shoulders sloping like lopped branches. It was done. I waited for the relief. But all I could think of was I'd be alone again.

'Touch? I was going to hit you. As for the touching. Forget it.' He went to the wardrobe and got down a case. 'You talk to Rolf tomorrow. Tell him there's no call for you working nights any-more, since Harry won't be here to bother you.' He began to pack methodically, then stopped, his blue-striped shirt in his hands. 'Jeez, I'd like to be here when old Rolf tries to make it with you.'

I closed my eyes to wait it out.

'Could work out though. Being screwed by a shrink. You might actually get to like it.' He twisted the shirt and flung it into the case. 'If he manages to cure you, gimme a call. Who knows? If I'm free, I might just come on over. Sample the fruits.'

'You can go fuck!'

He snapped the case shut. 'My sentiments exactly, honey. I plan on making up for lost time.'

'You're sick!'

' 'N you're really something else!' His tone held the same ugly note it had for months. He sat down abruptly on the stool before the mirror. Me and my big mouth. Then he laughed, a peculiar breathless sound that had no voice. 'Guess you're right. A man who's had his balls cut off is sick enough.'

'I don't want to hear.'

'That's your trouble.' He stood up. 'It's not a man you need, it's a goddamn machine.'

'I'll phone the movers, get them to deliver your stuff to the apartment.'

'Keep it.' He swiped his jacket. 'Or you'll have nothing.'

'You don't have to. I can get some second-hand.'

'With what?' He lifted the case and swung around. 'Your pension?'

'I'll manage.'

'So throw it out. All of it. I don't frigging want it, you hear?' He headed towards the door, then paused. 'I'll pay the rent for another month. After that you're on your own.'

I shouldn't have looked at him.

'For Christsake Em, how'd it get to this?'

I burrowed deeper into the quilt. But he waited.

'It was always ... difficult.' I said it as carefully as I could.

'Don't lie to me. It's ever since you joined that Centre. Listening to those freaks on the phone.'

He was closing in. But he was only half right. It was ever since their voices woke me to it.

'Don't forget your golf clubs. And your books —?'

'Read yourself a bedtime story!' The door crashed behind him. I listened to see if Eve would wake and heard the front door close quietly enough. The sound of the car retreating. Even the rain seemed quiet. I let go the quilt as the shuddering began in me. But I couldn't find the remote control. I dragged everything from the bed. It wasn't there. Had he taken it? The bastard must have taken it. He knew I didn't know how to operate the set. When I was on my knees searching, I spotted it on top of the television. Running over, I pressed the switch. The screen winked and Doctor Prince came instantly. I curled up on the jumbled clothes and concentrated until my eyes wouldn't stay open any longer. The children found me there in the morning.

'Did you wet the bed, Mommy?' Eve was goggle-eyed.

I tried to laugh. 'No I ... just had ... couldn't sleep, that's all.'

'Harry's gone.' Tom stared at the baseball bat. I couldn't answer him.

'Gone? Where? You never said. Harry always tells me so's I can ask him to bring me back a treat. You never said.' She began to cry.

'He's not coming back.' Tom kept his eyes on the bat.

'He is too! Isn't he Mommy? Isn't he?'

I couldn't face it. 'Yes, yes. Of course. C'mon. Move it or you'll miss the bus. Tom, go start breakfast. You, missy, get dressed.' I hustled them out. 'Hurry!'

Eve's voice carried back to me. 'You're real mean, saying that. Just 'cos you don't like Harry. I think he's neat.'

But Tom stayed silent.

———

I never noticed his silence growing. As I had Jack's. The rain was merciless in those weeks, pausing long enough to gather momentum, then drumming again, feeding me the beat of the voices, but always the sickness of her words soaking through to pound in a heavy rhythm. Rolf said she was out of the clinic, calling most nights. I read every report, unable to stop feeding on it. And though I now worked mornings, my hand shook each time I picked up the phone. But I had Doctor Prince to keep her out before I tried to sleep.

When the call came from the school, I couldn't handle it. Rolf went to see them. Then he talked to Tom.

'Well?' Sitting opposite his immaculate desk, I resisted the urge to light another cigarette. He was watching, his grey crew cut on the alert.

'He's pretty uncommunicative at school. His work is suffering. What's he been like at home?'

'Great. He doesn't argue with Eve anymore. Spends a lot of time in his room. Studying.' I looked back over the weeks. Then I saw it. 'He's gone very quiet. Only speaks if I ask him something. What's wrong with him?'

'He's grieving.'

'Grieving?' I stared at him. 'But Jack's been dead for years.'

'Christ, Emma. I'm talking about Harry!'

'Harry? I don't know what you —'

'Harry. The man you've been living with. What's up with you?' His eyes were too shrewd.

'What about the remote? The way he uses it?' I made a play of lighting a cigarette.

He shrugged. 'Gives him a sense of control.'

'Control?'

'Sure. He couldn't handle you and Harry. But he can push buttons whenever he likes.'

'He was doing it long before Harry left.'

'Yeah, ever since you and Harry began fighting?'

I stared out the window.

'What'll I do?'

'Nothing. At the moment he resents you both. He's going to see the school shrink. That, and time should do it. What I'd like to know is, what's eating you?'

'Me? I'm okay. I'm just missing Harry I suppose.'

'Bullshit. It was Jack you thought of straight off. Tom couldn't have been more than three.'

'I just got confused, that's all. Eve's started thumb-sucking again. D'you think —?'

'Tell me about Jack. What'd he die of?'

I jumped up. 'For God's sake, Rolf, a slip of the tongue. Leave me be, will you?' I managed a shaky laugh. 'I came to talk about Tom, remember?'

'It's time you talked about you. What's bugging you.'

'I'm fine. Nothing's bugging me. Except you.'

'Then talk to someone else. I've a friend, first-rate therapist. I'll arrange it.'

'I don't believe this! No, wait. That's not true. You've always looked at me as though ...'

'As though?'

'Nothing. Maybe you'd better get someone else.' I was edging towards the door when he spoke.

'Might be just as well. I was going to suggest you take a break.'

That stopped me. 'You're firing me?'

'Don't go putting words in my mouth, Emma.'

'That's what it boils down to!'

'You need help!'

'And you don't? You must've got through every woman in the place by now. You're the one that needs help.'

'Except you.' He grinned. 'Be fair to me.'

'I wouldn't touch you with a bargepole.'

'I wasn't inviting you to, sugar. I can't afford to risk swimming with a lame duck. Not in this line. Now, you want me to call this guy?' His hand hovered over the phone.

'Sure. Why not?'

'Terrific.' He was smiling.

'Tell him it's still raining.' I ran out, taking with me his open mouth and his thick finger arrested over the button.

I was at the bottom of the stairs when his roar made me turn. He was leaning over the banisters. 'Call me if you need.'

But I didn't.

In the beginning it was strange, not going to the Centre. I couldn't sleep in the raining dark that carried her voice, her words amplifying, almost drowning out the others. I began to doze out the mornings and spend the nights with Doctor Prince.

Doctor Prince looked like Jesus. I didn't believe in Jesus but I liked his pictures. Except for the one of the cross. Hanging fleshed to die. Doctor Prince was not flesh. He had a bland, translucent face with waterlogged eyes that demanded nothing. His long hair was the colour of rain clouds. His voice was bland, southern. When he switched to the recording of the black gospel woman singing 'Jesus is calling me', was when he went to the toilet. I went then too. Usually I was back in bed before he returned.

'Ain't nobody you can find as loyal to y'all as your Doctor Prince.' He always said the same thing when the song ended. 'My station is run from eight in the evening till eight in the morning and to those of you tuning in for the first time I say welcome. I'm here to bring you the words of Jesus, to bring the light of Jesus into your lives. Ain't no other TV station that offers you as much. No sir, no mam. Ain't no man of God willing to stay awake long as I do to bring you the love of Jesus. Now folks, if I'm to keep this here window open unto God's world, I can't do it on a shoestring, y'gotta show faith in your Doctor Prince by helping him under-write his TV ministry. All you gotta do is take that phone in your hand and call this here toll-free halo flashing over my head. All I'm asking is your pledge of fifteen dollars, or more from those who got it to spare, to help me beam the message of Jesus into your home. In return you'll receive your very own twenny-four K gold-plated "Jesus Power" badge and a prayer request card which you just fill in and return to my Prayer Warriors. They'll do the praying for you in perpetuity. And now, as I drink this here coffee, let us salute together, "King Jesus, Star of the Firmament".'

But I couldn't stop her coming in the haze of the mornings when Doctor Prince was sleeping, when I was too tired to drive to the market for groceries. Still it rained. We began to run out of things. Tom made us go to the store at night to get most of what we needed for the week. We went back to sugared cereals and granola bars for breakfast.

The first time Tom found the washing powder in the fridge, he laughed. After that, he just put it back on the shelf over the machine. Only when Eve complained about the streak of dye on her tee shirt, the tightness of her sweaters coming from the dryer, did it get through to me that Tom was doing the washing.

I couldn't stop it. I hated it, but I couldn't stop. One day I forgot to pick them up. The stop was only a half mile from the house, but they never walked it. Too many children had disappeared that way. It was the continuous harping of the phone that drew me away from her voice. The bus had a last run to make and they'd returned to school with it when I hadn't showed. I could hardly drive I was shaking so much. Call me if you need said Rolf cutting through the terror of what might have happened. And I would. Tonight. I would tell him about the sleeplessness. The tiredness. The forgetfulness. Nothing else. Nothing else. Doctor Prince would help me. First I would fill my mind with him. Then, when I was calm, I would phone.

But Doctor Prince never came. I stared at the blank screen, willing him to come. After a while a message showed. 'Doctor Prince apologises.' I waited some more, hoping. A long time later the screen filled with words: 'Doctor Prince regrets he is unable to be with you tonight. Doctor Prince would like you to know that the sabotage of his angel station in the sky is the direct work of his enemy the devil.' The bastard! I began throwing things about the room. How could he do this to me? He was always there. Always. Keeping me from it.

I called the Centre three times. A female voice. The fourth time I got Rolf. The words rose, stuck in my throat.

'Take your time. No hurry. Got all night if you want.' The soft tone he reserved for callers. 'You feeling low?'

Yes Rolf. Talk to me like that. Talk to me. And my words will come. Listen to me Rolf. I didn't want to remember. I didn't want to. But the voices made me. And Harry. Harry made me, his flesh quivering in a shrill parody. So I have to tell. I have to tell you. About Jack. Jack who hanged himself. Rolf, Rolf, d'you hear me? But the words stayed inside, choking.

'That's it. Let it out.'

Something burned down the coldness of my face. I tried to speak but my throat was swollen, gargling the words.

'Try and take a deep breath, so's you can talk. Alice ... it is Alice ... isn't it? C'mon, talk to me.'

Alice! I opened my mouth to scream but no sound came. I watched my hand smashing the receiver against the phone 'till it split. When I put it to my ear again Rolf was gone. Only silence and the drum on the roof. I sat there for a long time. Knowing. Why she had shouted in me. Then the calmness came. Simple. So simple. It was only the blindness that brought the fear. Now that I could see, I was no longer afraid. I went to the living room and slid back the glass door. The wet flagstones were cold under my feet. I stood under the rain and my eyes peeled the garden, layer by layer until it was arranged as that other garden, the stout branch conspiring to support his jerking weight. Then I put the layers back and stared at the space between the pear trees and the black hedge. That nothing place, that bituminous shadow webbed in rain. It was mine. I looked at it for a long time.

'My mind is a house,' I said to it. 'I have opened it to so many, there is no place for me to sleep. You must welcome me when I come.'

I went inside and stripped off the soaking nightgown. When I was dressed I sat at the kitchen table, planning it. After the children were gone I would visit each room. I was alert, filled with it. The peace that would come. Alice's voice no longer whispered in the hum of the rain. There was no need. My voice was strong. Poor Alice. You are a dodo. You run to the edge but you do not have conviction. Stay in your room, Alice, and call, call, call.

At breakfast I told the children they would go to Illinois for Thanksgiving, that I would follow. I watched their faces and knew it would be okay. Jack's parents couldn't see enough of them. It was a talking breakfast, like when Harry was around. They caught my mood, smelled the change, and were happy. I had five days to restore something of it.

The jewellery Harry had given me raised quite a lot. Not near what it was worth, but more than enough to pay for our tickets. After school I took them to the market.

'You really mean it, Mom?' Eve gripped the handle.

'Really. Whatever you like. But remember, maximum's twenty items. Okay. You got two minutes. Starting now!'

They shot off, their faces red, veering trollies in separate directions. My children. It is the bright things you must remember.

Eve returned first, laden with sweetstuff: meringues, desserts, crisps, cakes. Then Tom. I stared at the harvest of fruit, the vegetables. Tom. You are not remote. Already you are more than me. It is good.

'I knew what Eve'd choose. We have to ... ' He stopped.

'Yes, yes, you're right. We have to. But not even a tub of toffee ice-cream? Go get one.'

When I handed them over to the staff escort at the airport, I did not waver. They would thrive in Illinois. Here they will wither in my shadow. As I had done in his.

I am back at the house now, and have loosened the small pins that secure the windshield wipers. It has stopped raining. While I wait for the call to say they've arrived, I visit the rooms, hearing the voices speak with the tone of his hopelessness.

The last room I visit is Jack's. Its silence leaps at me through the closed door. I am a long time in that room.

The call has come.

I can destroy this house. Make it crumble in a quiet implosion when I drive the car from the breathless bends of Mount Talmalpais. Still I must wait. The rain does not fall yet, the rain that has given me my voice.

The garden sheds a lustre that is overbright. Under the fruit trees I hear the roots rustle in a wet burial as other roots have strained to hold him stifled. But from these roots have come the fruits we picked all summer: like Tom's, a choice of leafy green renewals. The thought is in, takes root before I know it, becomes entangled in the snarl of what is there.

When the rain begins, I lift my face to the first faltering drops.

The Immigrant

He went to the Haretons' barbeque alone, defiant in the face of her continued stubbornness. Normally, when they attended such functions they drifted apart, but he always felt comfortable having her somewhere in the background.

Now, he found he couldn't enjoy any of it, though he was damned if he'd go home early. He wandered among the tanned, garden faces, chatting idly, drinking too much, tired repeating the same information. As though she were uppermost in everybody's mind.

'Suzie not here?' Edna stared up at him, as glassy-eyed as he felt.

'That's the fourth time you've asked.'

'Is it?' She laughed. 'Must be the booze. 'Sides. Unusual to catch you on your own.' She'd paused deliberately before saying 'catch'. While she fished an olive out of her drink, he flicked his gaze over the Rubens-plump body, suddenly tempted.

Stretching up on tiptoe, she put a hand on his arm, her words tingling against his cheek. 'Gimme a lift home?'

He began to sweat, knowing it wasn't just the heat of the Australian sun on his fair skin.

'I, eh, was planning'n staying a little longer.'

'No hurry. I want to talk to Jimmy anyway. Lemme know when you're ready.'

She moved away, her scent ebbing from his nostrils. Taunting him. Christ. He'd enough to worry about without adding that. Still. A boost to the ego, in the face of Suzie's lack of interest, he couldn't deny it. Just nice to know somebody actually fancied you. Even if it had to be someone like Edna, who'd been around.

He watched her now, being pulled down to join a dappled group sprawled in the shade of a eucalyptus tree. With the usual crowd from the bank, the whole party was beginning to smack of a staff meeting. Hardly a face he didn't recognise, yet hardly a face he could claim really to know. Nodding and grinning and feeling foolish, he squeezed through the bulk of bodies congregated around the sizzling barbeques, his stomach heaving against the smell of roasting meat.

Outside on the street, his car smouldered in the full face of the sun. Shit. If only he'd thought to park it under a tree. The steering wheel stung his fingers. Fighting the impulse to open the window, he switched on the air conditioning. A year out of Ireland, he still found it hard to break old habits. The mirror leered, his mouth clenched in the inane grin he'd been wearing all afternoon. Damn Suzie! Doing it to spite him, he was sure of it. She'd never wanted to emigrate in the first place. And now she was going to make him pay. He should go home and have it out with her, that's what he should do.

Instead, he drove toward the harbour, parking at one of the vantage spots overlooking the opera house. Weekend Sydney in full swing, the myriad flecks of sail on an ocean of stippled glass. To return to the flat this soon would look like defeat. But the car was stifling, his sweat trickling faster than the seconds. He rammed the key into the ignition.

———

The apartment was empty, a hastily scribbled note on the kitchen table: 'Gone to Tontin — back about nine. If you open the balcony, be sure to keep the screen door closed — S.'

'S.' — the cool initial of an office memorandum. And Tontin. The aboriginal shacks outside the city. So. She hadn't given up.

Four hours to kill before she'd return. He stood, indecisive. Go back to the barbeque and flirt with Edna? Edible Edna. He laughed loudly, the room suddenly tense with stillness when the last echo died.

He went through to the bedroom and lay down. The silence was killing. He flicked the remote control and a welter of images blinked, forcing him to close his eyes against the glare of the screen.

———

'Michael? You asleep?'

The room was flickering. She stood, a black silhouette framed in the light from the passageway.

'You watching something?'

'No.' He fumbled for the control. When he finally pressed the button, the television disappeared as cleanly as if it'd never existed. Her voice came at him out of the dark. 'Is it still there, d'you think?'

'What?'

'The TV. Do we shape the picture, or does it shape us —?'

'Very funny —'

'The aboriginals believe, well, if a tree falls in the forest —'

'Hocus-bloody-pocus. What time's it?'

She stayed silent so long he thought she wasn't going to answer.

'Ten. I've put the kettle on. You want a cuppa?'

'Bit late, aren't you?'

She turned, moving down the corridor, her shadow sliding across his body. He reached out, grasping a fistful of shadow-hair as it slipped over the side of the bed. He tugged at it viciously, but already the shadow was racing away, vanishing under her heels as she walked directly beneath the light. A stupid thing to do; just as well she hadn't witnessed it.

The brightness in the kitchen made him squint. 'We have to talk.' He stared at the steaming mugs of tea.

Her small laugh grated. 'You've stolen my line.'

'Just how long more're you going to keep this up?' His spoon ground against the bottom of the cup.

'What?' Her face hidden by the dark swathes of hair — since when had she begun wearing it loose?

'What d'you mean "what"? How long more're you planning going out there? Christ, it's a wonder you haven't come home crawling with lice and fleas already!'

'I'm giving in my notice tomorrow.'

He turned away to hide the hugeness of his relief, his voice shaky. 'Well, I'm glad you've finally seen things —'

'At the bank. I meant at the bank.' Each word, evenly weighed, stabbing at his back.

He swivelled. 'You can't be serious —!'

'Never more.'

He tried to look into her eyes, but they were set, like small ice-blue chips of stone. He sat, winded. When his breathing was easier, he spoke. 'So you're going home.'

'Home?' She looked at him, amazed. 'Of course not. I'm going to work at the mission clinic.'

In the silence which followed, the wall clock ticked into existence, racing towards a future he couldn't quite grasp.

'Mike? Did you hear me?' Small, pale fingers touched his bare arm. He leapt up as though she'd scorched him. 'Of course I bloody heard! You're insane, you know that?'

'It's what I want.' She raised her hand. For a moment he thought she'd bite her nails but instead she tossed her hair back.

'When did you stop?' He stared at the neat cuticles, the uniform white tips.

'Oh, ages ago.' The light caught the glistening nails as she spread her fingers.

He searched the placid face, craving a glimpse of the girl he'd known, the nervous, homesick girl he'd had to drag to Australia, promising a trip home soon as they could afford it.

'You don't hate it here anymore, do you?' He tried to keep the surprise from his voice.

'No.'

The word jarred. Normally, she'd have answered with a dozen elaborations.

'Well, do tell what led to such a miraculous transformation? It can hardly be the climate, you've done nothing but moan about it since we arrived.'

He watched the dark stain spreading upwards across her cheeks and was glad.

'Look, you were the one who wanted to come here. I didn't. Naturally, it takes time to adjust —'

'Adjust?' His voice squeaked, a painful echo of adolescence. 'Leaving a well-paid job to go work in that, that rat-infested ...

cesspool!' He paced the kitchen, shoes clapping the stone tiles.

'If you really believe Tontin's a cesspool, then you should be ashamed!' She stood, her gaze instantly molten.

'What the hell's that supposed to mean? Well?'

Suddenly she wilted. 'Look, I'm jaded. We'll talk tomorrow.'

'No-no, do go on!' He strode to the open door, blocking her as she tried to exit. 'This I've got to hear, Reverend Mother's Lecture-Hour.' He bowed his head in mock piety.

'Don't do this, Mike.'

But her plea only fuelled his anger. 'So go on then Mother Teresa, tell me what I am!'

'Piss off!'

He had difficulty getting his tongue to work. 'Wh-what did you say?'

'You heard me.' She stood, her cotton blouse heaving, hands curled into cannons at her sides. 'If you don't like what I'm doing, you can frigging-well lump it!' She pushed past him into the passageway.

Suzie meek and Suzie mild. He stared after her, confounded. In a moment she'd entered the bathroom, the door slamming in her wake. Then the shower was running, its echo tinkling forever in the kitchen drain. Later, the discreet flush of the toilet carried back to his ears. For a long time he stood, afraid to analyse any of it, the sharp contours of the space-age kitchen shutting him out.

She was asleep when he eased in beside her, the familiar whiff of her skin making him ache.

———

The days erupted in a spillage of words with long spells of silence in between becoming lulls in which he gathered strength for his next onslaught. At night they slept, rigidly apart, even in the depths of sleep. But he couldn't wear her down.

At the bank, his uncle called him to his office.

'Is she mad, or what?'

Mike stuffed his fists safely in his pockets as he stared down from the window, the pavement fourteen floors below, a convulsive assembly line of dwarves.

'It wasn't easy pulling jobs for the both of you. Jobs like this don't grow on —'

'I know.'

'So what's the story?'

Mike turned. Twenty years down the line, the map of veins on his uncle's cheeks was still doing battle with a foreign climate.

'Your guess's good as mine,' he blurted.

His uncle's face softened. 'Teething troubles, lad. Every marriage has them. Just talk some sense into her, she's a great little one behind it all.'

'I've done talking. It's her lookout. Anyway, she's a mind of her own,' he added, suddenly realising it was true. For the first time he felt afraid.

'If y'ask me, she's half-cracked, giving up a good position —'

'Well, I didn't!' Mike strode out of the office.

————

That evening, he asked the question his uncle's interference had prompted.

'Did you tell any of them?'

'What?' She'd changed into a pair of shorts before dinner. He avoided watching her legs flitting between table and sink as she cleared up.

'About the ...' he chewed on the word distastefully '... clinic.'

'One or two.'

'Who?'

Water drummed in the steel bowl. 'Maisie in Foreign Exchange.'

'Could you at least turn that off?' He jerked a hand towards the tap. 'Who else? Did you say anything to "Round-the-fire"?' The nickname they'd bestowed on his uncle slipped out. Instantly he was sorry, afraid she'd take it as a gesture of intimacy, a weakening of his resolve.

'I saw no point. He was livid enough.'

Mike was relieved. The less he had to explain the better. His gaze dropped to the curve of her buttocks in the shorts. She'd put on a little weight. It suited her. He shifted uncomfortably in his business suit. When she came again to the table, without planning to, he found himself reaching out shakily, pulling her onto his lap.

'Let's go to bed,' he said, hiding his expression in her hair. 'Before we both forget what it's like.' He tried to laugh, but the sound crumbled in his ears.

'I, I couldn't.' She stared woodenly across his left shoulder. 'There's been so much ... it'd be a mockery ...'

The humiliation burned somewhere deep in him. He slackened his hold, and immediately she stood. Immediately. As if she couldn't stand—. 'Mockery? Christ that's good, that's rich, that is!'

'It wouldn't solve anything, and you know it!' She swiped the last of the plates with a clatter.

'You're chipping them.'

'So bloody what! You've been chipping away at me for months and nothing of it!' She flung them in the sink. Water rose in a burst of spray to slap on the tiles.

'We're going to find it hard enough managing on my salary without you breaking the fucking dishes!'

She stared at him. 'What're you saying —?'

'What about the house we were going to buy? Y'think we'll be able to afford that now?'

'There's nothing wrong with this place —'

'What if we have kids —?' He could have bitten his tongue out.

'Don't give me that crap. Everytime I brought up the subject, you buried it. You don't want kids, Mike. You want *things!* — a plush house, a fancy car —'

'So? It's what everybody —'

'It's not what I want! I'd ... suffocate!'

'Well, fat chance of me getting it while I have to support you and your madcap schemes!' His breathing punctured the long silence.

'So that's it, that's really what it's all about?'

He tried not to wince at how shocked she sounded.

'I should've realised, I've become a, a ... liability.' There was a small, muffled sound, but he wouldn't raise his head to look at her.

When she spoke again, her voice was cold. 'You know, the one thing I find it hard to forgive is what you put us through to come to this.' Her thin laugh scraped the quiet. 'Imagine! I'd no idea, really no idea that this was what it was, ah, what the fuck does it matter now, anyhow!' She moved towards the door. 'I'll move out Friday, when I finish at the bank.'

He almost laughed, sure of his ground. 'Don't be daft, where could you go? You'd soon run out of money —'

'Tontin. The clinic runs to bed and board for the volunteers who need it.'

He stared after her, struggling with it as he heard her moving about the bedroom. In a few quick strides he could undo it. He half-rose, then sat again. If he went to her now, he would have to accept what she was doing. He could not. Nor could he face the why of it, baulking at the question, part of his mind detaching itself, infusing him with a logic of its own. Living in that hell-hole would be a far cry from her weekend visits. Why not let her? In a few weeks, days even, she'd be back, the whole thing flushed out of her system. Perhaps it was the best thing after all.

———

He missed her. Several times he was tempted to drive out to Tontin. Instead, he called Edna, went drinking in various bars. It didn't help much, but he hated the emptiness of the flat. He kept it excessively tidy in case she returned, wanting her to witness how well he was managing.

Once, after shaving, he found himself rinsing the enamelled sink in an awkward, clockwise motion, having unconsciously assumed her habit. He stood staring at his moving hands, unable to stop, as though imitating her gestures would somehow bring her closer. The large tube of toothpaste they'd shared was almost empty. He hadn't bought another one in the perverse belief that she'd return before it ran out. He tried not to look at it now as it sagged over the lip of the tumbler with all the dejection of a crushed witness, his toothbrush listing beside it like a drunken flagpole. When the tattered bristles blurred suddenly, he realised he was crying. In a fit of rage, he tore through the flat, changing all the furniture about.

One night he brought Edna home, but he was too drunk to make love to her. When he awoke, he was alone, stripped to his underpants under the coverlet. He shied away from the hazy recollection of his clumsy hands plundering her body. She must have put him to bed.

The next evening he drove aimlessly from the hilly, harbourside suburbs, northwards through the city towards Taronga Park. The air had cooled sufficiently to admit a fresh breeze through the car window. Everywhere, lawn sprinklers hissed, soaking the well-groomed gardens.

What was it she'd said? 'When y'think of the bogs back home, it'd make you laugh.'

Bogs. The small, mildewed farm subsiding in the maw of those grim quagmires, the bitter-brown mulch of decayed centuries sucking his strength, he'd been lucky to escape the dank history of such a place.

His resolve suddenly crumbled. Turning the car back towards the coast, he took the road to Tontin. Long before he reached it, he caught the ripple of sunset in the corrugated roofs scattered like nuggets about the makeshift church. Two long low Porta-Cabins, she'd said, standing in the lee of the church, that's where he could find her. If he ever wanted to. If he ever changed his mind.

Close up, the place was a ghetto. He parked the car on the outskirts, locking it securely. Foolhardy to attempt navigation of the rutted sandy track which served as a road between the miscellany of patched tin huts.

There was no footpath. He set out, gingerly avoiding the craters riddling the track. Here and there, he was aware of low voices, people sitting in the dusty yards, the broken wire of fences trailing in clumps of scrub grass. He kept his eyes averted. A child's laughter rang out, startling him. Surreptitiously he glanced at the pathetic neatness of the yards, the bins covered with bits of rusted corrugate to keep the flies out. Once or twice, passing shadowy alleys that rustled with life, his skin bristled. Passing a row of tin latrines, he stopped breathing to block the stench of excrement. Ahead, close to the church, people queued at a communal pump for water.

He turned in at the cabins, coming upon her suddenly as she sat in the coarse grass rocking a dark, fat baby with odd thatches of bristling, matted hair. The setting sun at her back. His lips twisted. Apt, that, a fucking benediction. About her, a tight-knit group of women leaned towards her, their faces absorbed. Coming closer, he realised she was correcting their English. A little distance away, a silver-haired priest squatted with a group of aboriginal men.

'I ... just wondered how you were,' he said awkwardly as she looked up at him. Wordlessly she handed the child to one of the women and he saw what he'd missed in the baby, the ballooning stomach, the listless eyes below bald patches of scalp, sights he'd only ever seen on TV. He turned away, unable to stomach it in the flesh.

She walked with him to the car.

'D'you have enough? Money, I mean.' He stumbled in a rut, almost pitching forward, already sorry he'd come.

'You'll never complain about an Irish pot-hole after this,' she laughed. Her cheerfulness stabbed him.

'How do you get supplies in?'

'Oh, we manage,' she said airily.

The 'we' annoyed him. He stuffed his hands in his pockets, kicking at the tyres.

'Listen, we would've split up eventually, you know that, don't you?' Her voice was gentle. He nodded, his throat clenched. Somehow he got the words out.

'But you used this place as an excuse.'

The sudden blush dyeing her cheeks was balm to his wound. They stood for a while, unable to look at each other, the pain between them swelling the silence 'till he thought he would burst. When at last she spoke, her voice was quiet.

'Nobody's to blame. We just wanted different things.'

There on the shadowy edge of those hovels, the sun going down fast, it hit him, everything he'd refused to analyse.

'Mike? Are you okay? You look —' She reached out to touch him and he hugged her fiercely.

'You'll come again?' she asked when he released her. He nodded, but they both knew he wouldn't. She'd asked the question merely to camouflage the finality that rested concrete as a mountain between them.

Driving away, he looked in the mirror to catch a last glimpse of her, but the dust had risen like a fog bank, effectively screening her and the whole tin-town at her back.

———

He stared through the balcony window at the distant body specks on Bondi Beach.

'Come back, too soon to get up,' Edna's drowsy voice carried from the bed.

'In a minute.' He glanced at the careless sheet draping her body with classic abandon. It didn't move him. Turning, he looked outside again.

Suzie. Shades of her concern reaching deep into him.

No. They couldn't have stayed together. The instinct to drive her out had been one of self-preservation. His skin hadn't sustained the centuries of evolution possessed in the dark, inalienable faces of Tontin. He was immigrant. Only that. To know himself by any other name, would be to admit shame into the vacuum he'd carefully nurtured.

He stood, wishing he were one of the body specks crowding the beach, the sun driving the shadow of Suzie back among the corrugated rocks. Tomorrow, he'd have to buy some toothpaste.

The Note

I wonder at the need I have to write this now. It is too late for such an exercise to be therapeutic. Much too late. Could it be that I wish to form a clear picture in my mind of why we have come to this exact point? Perhaps that is why I am making this attempt to record something of our time together.

I think that is it, but I am not sure yet.

It is strange that I am still. Like the ice that holds the lake outside this window, though a change is coming. Already the melting slivers plunge into the slurry beneath as the slow thaw begins.

The house is quiet. There is only the scratch of these words fusing with the page to melt the silence. Soon I will hear something of his movements. But not yet.

I write slowly, hindered by the pictures that rush in, glutting my vision.

But it is late. I must choose. Already the sun is slinking from this room and if I do not get enough time to record it all then at least I should speak of our beginning.

My memory is good. Focusing, I wonder why every detail of that first meeting should be so clear in my mind after all this time? (Perhaps the answer will present itself like some thoughts do, unbidden, when I least expect it.) But for now it is enough that I remember.

I can still see the hot chocolate stall squatting on the ice several yards out from the shoreline. When I first saw him, he was sitting in the wheelchair near the stall staring out across the frozen lake.

Even then he did not make it easy for me.

I skated off, returning in a fluster for a second drink when some time had passed. I was twenty-two then. And broke. I had two more nights to go in the hostel for homeless women. The skates were my last valuable possession. A woman in the pawn shop on the corner of Kalverstraat, I remember, had promised me forty guilders for them when I would most need the money.

Never before that moment had I contemplated singling out a man. The old fellow behind the steamy counter stared at me as I moved slowly towards the wheelchair, the peaty liquid in the plastic cup warming my hand.

He sat motionless, oblivious to the scrape of my skates, the blades shaving thin streams of powdered ice as I approached. When I stood before him he would not look at me. I was forced to speak before he shifted his gaze. Even then I hated him, much as he drew me. He had a way of flicking his eyes upwards while keeping his massive head rigid that still reminds me of the alertness of an animal who senses his prey.

'Would you like some?' My Dutch was halting, awkward with the weight of embarrassment.

'No. I hate the stuff.'

I closed my mouth, clamping on the urge to apologise as I turned away.

'It's too sweet. Cloying.'

The English words drew me back to stand self-consciously before him.

'How old are you?' His question niggled.

'Old enough.'

'Hm, maybe you are. Okay, let's cut the crap. We'll go to my house.'

My mouth dropped open.

'What's the matter? Thought because I'm a cripple I couldn't manage it? I'd be a soft touch?'

'But I'm not ... You think I'm a ...?' I was too confused to do more than splutter.

'Whore? Of course. What other kind of female is interested in a cripple? But be warned. You'll get no busman's holiday with me. Apart from my legs, all other parts of my anatomy function normally. Well?'

The heavy shoulders lifted as he flicked a switch and the small motor whirred.

'Piss off.' Shaking, I turned, the chocolate spilling on the ice, its dark colour frosting in a congealed mess. I was glad he was in the wheelchair but the efficient sound of the motor worried me. I began to skate away quickly.

'Fucking tart.' His voice quivered with the angry thrum of the machine, stabbing the air at my back.

———

The next day I walked the four miles from the city again. The lake was crowded. A Saturday? There was slush about the chocolate stall where the top layer of ice had begun to melt in the heat generated by the steel vats. The old man was brushing away nonchalantly at the foundation which supported him. Cold as I was, I stopped to watch him. Standing there among all the movement and colour, the skaters twisting between the sleighs and go-carts, the surfboards skittering across the ice, I began to fear that I was melting like the ice about that stall, dissipating into the cutting, jabbing air.

Finally I caught sight of him. He had manoeuvred his wheelchair to push-start two boys in a low wooden pram with a make-shift mast and sail. The children's smiles died under his gaze. Then the cotton sheet ballooned in a gust of wind and the boys shrieked as the pram began to roll.

'Changed your mind?' The wheels screamed as he swung the chair to face me and his hand moved to kill the whine of the motor.

'I've no place to stay.'

'I don't rent rooms.' The words snapped like cracking ice.

'I didn't mean that. I've no money anyway.' I tried to concentrate on the blur of moving figures on the lake.

'Nothing's ever free.'

'I'm not a prostitute.' But my protest was feeble, crippled by the need to be with someone, the need that had driven me towards him.

'Then it's time you got started.'

———

That then, was how we began with one another, our beginning quickly spreading its contagion to a bond that, until now, has promised no remission.

Here, in his house south of the city I have lived for a long time staring out at the freeze and thaw, lap and flow of the lake as he sculpts behind me in the large room with its vaulted ceiling, the chisel singing in the stone, carving out the ugliness of our obsession. This room has been my prison, hated and loved and yes, even jealously guarded with the neurotic intensity only the prisoner can know.

Here I am interned in the remorseless granite of his sculptures: every shape, every stone bears some aspect I know, my hair on the grainy half-formed creature which leaps from a huge shard of rock as though blasted from the ceiling of the lake itself: my thin shoulders borne by the addict injecting himself; my breasts on the tired prostitute, and there, in the hand of the child, the finger on my left hand, the finger he broke in a fit of rage when Piet hugged me on New Year's Eve. Piet has never been to the house since, though he is still his agent. I know this because I found one of the catalogues from his last exhibition. Piet's name was on it. And I know when he talks to Piet on the telephone. His voice changes, becomes sharper, cold. It carries clearly through the thickset door, its tone undeniable though the words are rarely distinguishable.

We have lived between this room and two others on the ground floor, the kitchen and the library where we have slept among the mouldy books. There is another room at the back of the house overlooking the flatness of the polders, the room where the phone is, where he goes every morning usually before he thinks I am awake. This room I have never been in but sometimes I have tiptoed to the door and stood with my ear pressed to the cold wood. Listening. But never to the phone calls. It is the silences which make me curious. I am glad the phone is in that room, that I am never forced to answer it. I have always been afraid to answer it.

Once, he told me, my mother called. (I do not know how she tracked me down. I am a long way from where she lives.) Perhaps he was telling me the truth. I do not know. But I was glad when he told me what he said to her, even if it was not true. He said he made her swear never to come here, never to try to see me. He said he had this lawyer friend, that my stepfather could be put in jail, even now, such a long time after it all and that her name would be mud for ever afterwards because she is to blame as well, he said. But perhaps he was lying. It is difficult to know. Perhaps he made it up just to frighten me. He has often done that. As on New Year, after Piet had left. When he made the soup and fed it to me because my fingers were too swollen to hold the spoon. He was kind and gentle feeding it to me, making me drink every last drop, the way a mother would feed a sick child — a mother, I mean, who loved her child. Then he told me the soup was poisoned.

So perhaps that day he said my mother called, he was trying to frighten me. That is how he can be. Since I realised this, I have not been so frightened. I remember that night after the call, he wanted me to skate on the lake. The thaw had already set in along some parts of the shoreline and we had to go far out to find a part where the ice hummed solidly. There in the moonlight, I was afraid of the ice, afraid when he talked about the phone call. Sometimes when I try to understand why he wanted me to skate that night, I cannot think because my ears fill with the tinny cracks that stretched towards us as we made our way back to the shore in the white light.

The light is dying now and as I wait I can hear him preparing in his room, that room he guards so jealously from me.

The only other person he has allowed to enter it is Doctor Nieuwhuizen who has called each month to check his legs. I have been glad of the doctor's visits. Apart from quiet fat Anka who comes every day to clean for us and cook the main meal, there has been nobody else he will have call to the house.

I cannot write much more. Darkness leans on the page, weighs on my eyes. Is it because of this that my other senses become acute? I do not know. But I have become more aware of the acrid stonedust clogging my nostrils, settling in my throat, gritting my nails. I have been absorbed more and more by each new sculpture he has created, I have been diminished as each one has grown, I am suffocating among these hulking, icy statues.

Soon he will come for me as he has said (there is only truth now between us) and then at last it will end and that, I now know, is why I have felt this urgency, this need to sit and record something of us, something of our beginning since it has determined what our being together has been. (I can almost say 'was' for it is all almost over now.) There have been other women before me, women like me. He has told me little of them. But our end will speak for itself as the beginning does, brushing, brushing at the foundations which supported us. And there is my answer. It is because of the fear that I remember the beginning so sharply, the melting of the ice about that stall.

Already it is time. The thin scream of the motor stabs the silence as he approaches. When quiet fat Anka shuffles slowly into the house tomorrow she will read this with knowing eyes.

Chameleon

It is getting worse. When I visit the doctor, he is no help, dismissing my fears with his pin-striped shrug. 'You're a middle-aged man, body's slowing down a little,' he says. 'But your heart's quite normal, sound as a bell, in fact.' There is boredom in his poached eyes. He offers me tranquillizers, sleeping pills, a visit to a psychiatrist, even suggests a good holiday. 'You're working too hard, you should learn to relax.' In the quiet, his fingers drum the desk. You are dis-missed, they say, dis-miss-dis-missed. Still I sit, watching his mouth narrow to frame a polite goodbye, but instead he says, 'Have sex more often, good for the circulation.' He laughs. I cough to hide my embarrassment, unable to meet his face as he ushers me out.

In the street my eyes water, but it is not the sunlight, it is the sludge of my fear rising to blind me.

Though I was too ashamed to explain my condition to him, afraid he would think me mad, yet he was my one hope. If only his eye had fixed on something in me physically, a rash on my back perhaps, or a bone jutting out of place, something, anything, which would've entailed his giving me the right kind of treatment!

Now there is no one I can turn to. And it is getting worse, much worse. Lately, it has even been difficult to remember a time when it was not like this, a time when I was ... normal. Each ... chameleon-episode (that is what I call them, I know no other words which fit my strange condition), yes, each ... episode, leaves me weaker than before, less in control.

But I must document everything, then perhaps I can reason, make logic of it, for that is what helps a man to be himself. To *be himself*. There! — even thinking the words so positively, forcefully, gives me courage, for I know not when the next stage will strike, but stage it will be, for this ... thing, this condition of mine, has begun to develop a new pattern —. Oh I am almost afraid to entertain it, afraid my thinking about it will precipitate something so terrible, it will be beyond my cunning to contain! But I must not weaken, therein lies my destruction.

I must begin with the office party for it was after this the first episode occurred: Yes. I am ... watching my wife talking to the sales manager, yes, that's it, the exact point at which my heart first shudders. She is smaller than he, so he must bend a little to catch her drift. When he does this, his dark head looks ... perfect, I will have to say it ... perfect ... against her fair one.

'Is that De Burca's wife? Some dame!' sniggers Murphy, the new man. The way he says it makes me sweat, his breath rank against my cheek. I stare down at his shoes. Expensive leather, like De Burca's. I do not like Murphy. His mouth is arranged in a perpetual leer, as though he's found out some dirty secret about you, a secret even you don't know ... yet. This is the way he makes me feel now. I mumble something about the party going well. I am too embarrassed to claim my wife now she's been ... coupled ... with De Burca. I know if I claim her, it will widen the leer on Murphy's lips, making the secret he knows about me, larger ... even ... dirtier.

Later, when I am at home in my bathroom brushing my teeth, my wife already in bed pretending to sleep, I think about De Burca. And Murphy. I think about my wife. From the mirror, a man stares back, his mouth rabid with toothpaste, his face the tight blue tilt of, of rage ... of pain. I am not sure why he is so upset, why I can feel his anger growing until he is hurling his blue, buzzing madness against the walls. From the bedroom, my wife shrieks. She is telling me to come and swat the fly buzzing in her face. The air about me is displaced as she strikes out. Again and again she tells me to come, tells me why she wants me. But she does not have to tell me. I know. I know because I am not in the bathroom. I am in the bedroom. Buzzing about her face. My wife ... hates ... bluebottles. She is ... afraid ... of them.

In a little while I am back in the bathroom again, watching the tightness drain from the face in the mirror. This time I ... walk ... back into the bedroom. 'Did you call me?' I say it low, afraid my voice will reveal something ... I am not sure what ... but something ... strange.

'There was a fly, a big ugly —' She shivers, the quilt drawn up to her chin, her eyes out on stalks. 'Didn't you hear me?' I tell her the water was running. 'Can you hear it?' She cocks her head, her delicate hands pecking the sheet. But the room holds only the rasp of the clock. I pretend to search, I even shake the curtains which are never drawn because she loves to watch the moths tapping out their ritual against the lighted window. 'Maybe it's in the bathroom?' she says.

'No, I'd've heard it,' I say, climbing into bed. Lying there, listening to her breath filling the dark, I am calm, all the tightness drained from my body. That night, I sleep well. For several nights, the sleeping well continues.

But one day in my office, I yearn to be at home, I yearn to see my wife. I lean back in my swivel chair after I have finished the financial statements. I close my eyes. I imagine that I am not in my office. Instead I am walking round the side of my house to the back door, coming home as I always do in the evenings. I pretend I am a cat, sleek, magnificent, my fur a warm, pungent cocoon. I stop, coaxing a mote of dust from my right flank. I do this deliberately, to delay the pleasure of seeing my wife. When I can bear it no longer, I pad softly to the door, calling her. She does not come. I call again. The door opens, her cornflower eyes widening with delight as she looks down. She murmurs something, bending to stroke me, her fragrance deep in my nostrils. My wife loves cats. My back arches. In the depths of my throat, a lion purrs. She lifts me up, carries me inside. I curve against her, resting my head upon her softness. Oh ecstasy!

While I am lapping the milk she pours, somebody walks into the room. Somebody with expensive leather shoes. In my terror, I paw the saucer, spilling the milk across the tiles. The saucer spins out of orbit, then crashes down, a sliver striking my face. There is anger spitting, hissing all round me, in me. The shoes kick out. My wife tries to stop them. I streak through the open door, their voices giving chase, locked in a language I cannot understand. Suddenly, my secretary is shaking me. 'Where've you been?' she says. 'I've been up and down the building searching, you missed your appointment with De Burca this morning, he's piffed.' She trips to the open window, her perm bobbing. 'However did a cat get in your office?' She sniffs, peering down. 'Well, least he's not lying spattered on the pavement. Poor thing! Did you ever see such a leap, scared stiff he was when I walked in and found him curled in your chair. Lucky the window was open, don't know how you can leave it open when we're up so high, this place is like a fridge.'

From behind my hands, I mumble something about not feeling well, needing some air. But it is this episode which tells me the bluebottle was real, for later, when I go home, my wife asks what happened my face. 'I, I cut it, eh ... shaving,' I say, not looking at her. When I scrape my dinner-plate into the bin, it lands on shards of broken saucer.

That, then, is how it began, but the why of it still eludes me. I have spent months poring over scientific books, searching for some rational explanation. But science too is full of its own quantum uncertainties, whilst time and again I have been able to verify my condition, each new chameleon leaving behind its undeniable trail of clues. Yet lately I seem to have entered a new phase where I am no longer in control, times when I find myself changed, suddenly, without ever having willed it, each change proving more abhorrent to my wife. Though I fight it, each battle leaves me weaker, less able to shorten the time-span of the next episode. Last night at dinner I had to rush into the garden as I felt it coming, the same blue tightness that is now a warning sign. If it should happen before her eyes! I ran, her voice trailing me, saying something about the office, about De Burca, her tone light, as though she were speaking of springtime.

By the time she followed me outside, the change was complete, her screams choking the night as I leapt the box hedge. For hours I was forced to slink about the shadowy streets. Oh is there no hope for me?

Back now in my office, I stare at the small, shaky line I have drawn through the doctor's appointment in my diary. Although the pen is still in my hand, I am too tired to sign the letters on my desk, at this moment I cannot even be sure I know my own signature! The thought frightens me. Oh I must get out of this room, I must find somebody I can talk to! I hurry to open my door. Perhaps my secretary has come back from lunch, perhaps she'll greet me by my name.

Outside, Murphy is sitting on her desk, his hand deep under her skirt, the fabric rising and falling with the motion of his arm. Her back is stiff, her buttocks squeaking a little on the leather chair. Murphy sees me. Still looking at me, still kneading her, he bends low, whispering in her ear. She giggles, her words half-swallowed as she clutches his knee. But I am sure I hear her say my name. Murphy sniggers. I go back in my office, careful not to slam the door. Careful not to let him see I know he is laughing at me. I have to feel my way around my desk. Inside, a rage is growing. I want to ... kill ... Murphy. My secretary. De Burca. The rage makes me suck in air, breathe deeply, makes me strong. Tonight, oh, there will never be a chameleon to equal it, I will become a, a ... python, yes, oh yes, I want to squeeze my wife, I want to squeeze the breath out of her, keep on squeezing her forever. I did not think it possible but I am, I am strong again!

All afternoon my rage sustains me, all evening as I observe my wife while she watches television. Climbing into bed, I am shivering, the tightness so strong in me that I do not think I can contain it until she is asleep. Suddenly I feel her gaze on my face. 'Are you okay?' She half reaches out, as though she would touch me, her face ... distressed. This surprises me. I screw up my eyes to see better. Then ... yes, it is, her hand, cool on my brow, so gentle, so ... wanted! The touch of her skin draining my strength, draining my will to change. How, how could I think to harm her whom I love more than my breath! But the change has begun, its pulse leaping in me, oh I'll fight it, I will fight! If I must change then let it be something small, something infinitely light, I do not want to be a python, if I must be something, then let it be a, a ... moth, such fragility will please her. In summer, when there is one in the house, always she makes me cup its delicacy in my hands, return it to the night, oh yes, let it be a moth rising to the light, the unbearable sweetness of it!

Suddenly, the air about me thickens with the smell of panic, my wife's face blurring as she jumps from the bed, her voice garbled as though it has travelled a long way through water, oh don't go, don't leave me! Swiftly I follow as she rushes from the house out across the dark lawn, where, where are you going, what, what is it? I soar above her head, sensing the street lamp, its brilliance blistering the night. Like a magnet it draws me away from her, oh I cannot stop my ... gossamer winging ... to the light! On its warm sun I rest, willing my strength to return, to carry me back.

It is a long time before I can wrench free, before I find my way home. But the door of my house is closed. Through the window I see my wife. Our neighbour is stooped over our bed, his face shocked out of sleep as he mouths words. I cannot see what they are looking at beyond the mound of the quilt. I try, but I am too weak to climb higher on the glass, oh let, let me in, I am here!

At last my wife comes to the window. Look, look at me! I hurl myself against the glass, but she stares beyond me into the night. She reaches, drawing the curtains. Take into your hand my ... darkening eyes.

I cannot get back. I try to move, but I am no longer a moth, I am lighter, infinitely weaker. The doctor was wrong. A heart can ... burst ... Oh ... grief!

I look down at myself to see what I am.

There is ... nothing —

The Savage Sameness

I stood, gaping at it: the de-railed cattle-car of some ancient mid-western train, from which you'd expect an American hobo, stubble-jawed and grimy, to emerge with the weary eyes of the dispossessed.

Except this was Holland.

In the distance, on the grey rim of the polders, the first swell of sun had pierced the mist, defining the box-car, its brooding rectangle crouched in the centre of the field.

I was panting like a steam engine, twin arcs of sweat spreading under my breasts from the effort of the long walk to get here. Joachim stood beside me, silent. He had to be all of fifty, yet the way I was breathing it was hard to tell I was twenty years younger.

'This is where you live?' I looked up at him, hoping he'd deny it.

His head jerked in that peculiar habit he had, as though his neck had snapped. 'Ja.'

Itchy and disgusted, I wriggled against the clammy roughness of my jeans. 'Figures.'

'Zo?'

'S'got your wooden stare.' I spoke slowly, trying to keep the alcohol from my voice.

He didn't answer. Just walked ahead along the grassy track. From the canal bordering the field came the first rustles of water-fowl. I stood staring towards the sedge that screened the muttering water.

'Short distance' my ass — a two-mile stumble along the sodden dike, the night black as bitumen — his large paw grasping me upright every time I slipped, a wonder I hadn't drowned. All that effort to reach a crate in the middle of nowhere. Sod it.

'Komme! You are coming!' The sliding panel screeched as he hove it, the canal bank responding with a few nervous squawks.

The interior of the box-car gaped, darkness swallowing his bulk. Eejit, what was he proving, that he could rough it?

At my feet, a tuft of grass shimmered, the framework of a spider's web bleeding in the early light. I shivered, unwilling to move.

It should've dawned on me then, but it didn't. Even knowing something of his past, gossip I'd heard in the bar, still it never struck me why he'd chosen to live in such a thing.

He'd lit a lamp. No question of it being electric, not the way the bluish light seeped into the interior, a process of erosion that couldn't quench the darkness.

'Kom binnen! The door must be closed. I don't want bats in my house!'

Bats! My skin came alive, a thousand insects scrabbling across its surface. Head down, I ran along the track, a hoarse whistle from the bank making me scream. There was no step, no civilised method of getting inside. It still had its flanged wheels, the wooden floor level with my ribs.

'Give us a hand, will you?' I reached up. Instead, he bypassed, hauling my anorak by the neck. It rode upwards, half choking me.

'My blouse is jammed, what're you trying to do, throttle me?' I struggled with the zip, fumes of paraffin invading my nostrils.

'Why did you squeal?'

That got me. 'I didn't squeal, I ... shrieked. Pigs squeal.'

He grinned. 'I am cognizant of this fact.'

'Oh feck off, will you! Anything to drink?' As he moved across to a box on the floor, I looked around, then wished I hadn't. A camp bed folded in a corner. A makeshift table on which stood a miscellany, primus stove, dishes, pots, chisels, hand-mallets, other sculpting tools, a few books, and the lamp, its flame kicking in the glass womb. A bench before the table. In a corner, a curtain strung on twine. Clothes, maybe?

'I have only viskey.' He proffered the bottle.

'Whiskey?' I stared at the dark grooves below his eyes. 'Look, I may've been pissed in the bar tonight, but it doesn't mean I'm an alcoholic, whatever you might've heard about the Irish. What I'm looking for is coffee, if this ... ' I looked around, '... hotel, runs to such luxuries. I don't vant your viskey.' My mimicry sliced the air and I felt ashamed.

'Sorry, I'm sorry, it's just I'm banjaxed.' I scuffed the floor, raising a fog of dust.

'What means this word?' He struck a match, the flame hissing as he lit the primus.

'Wiped out.' I dragged across the boards, a uniform throbbing coming into its own as I sank onto the bench. Jesus. Like I had one huge foot. 'And don't ask me the origin, I'm not up to it. Besides, I don't know.'

Despite what I said, he began to speculate on the word as he made coffee, his voice growling against the wood. I said little. Now that I was sober I was kicking myself for having come. Our conversation seemed a camouflage, as though under its desultoriness we were beating round some bush, only it was his bush, a dark and thorny thing materialising in sporadic bursts through the swirling polder-mist. Yet it was I who was prickly. Afraid, almost.

When he couldn't draw me out, he too became silent, sitting on the table's edge, watching the vapor rise from the coffee.

I lit a cigarette, smoke snaking into the oiled air, forming a ceiling above our heads. It might've been the fog through which we'd hauled our way out here. Surrounding us now in this wooden box. I shivered. Why had he asked me to come? More to the point, when I'd a room of my own, why had I accepted? It'd nothing to do with sex. At least not yet. That he was offering me something was clear, but I didn't know what it was. Even when his eyes were wide open, they were veiled.

I ground the cigarette in a tin cluttered with nails. The grids set high in the creosote walls had begun to define the outside light, almost enough to see my way back to town. Whatever Joachim was offering, I didn't want it. After Mike's betrayal, I was still too raw to handle anything that didn't smack of monotony.

As though he sensed my decision, he strode to the bed, snapping it open. 'You can sleep here.' The mattress exposed a squashed sleeping bag.

'It's nearly daylight. I'll go back.' Standing, my feet mutinied.

'It's a long walk, you should rest. Later, we can eat. Then I'll take you back.' He paused for a moment. 'If you wish.'

The sleeping bag looked comfortable. 'Where'll you —?'

'On zi ground, a blenket.'

I was too tired to pretend protest. While he laid some plastic on the floor, I kicked off my sneakers and crawled into the bag, turning to the wall so I wouldn't have to look at him, whorls of wood gyrating before my eyes.

The sharp ring of metal against stone woke me: a relentless staccato the other side of the wood. What the hell was he doing? I moved slowly to minimise the pulsing in my head. My teeth were layers of fungus and I needed to pee. The lamp no longer glowed, dust spinning in the narrow sunlight shafting the grids, reinforcing the surrounding gloom. The drumbeat in my head quickened in time to the singing stone. Whole centuries passed before I was outside, dragging round the back to where he stood, dark hair greying as he sculpted.

'D'you have to?' My voice was gravel dredging a parched well. He spun around, the chisel in his hand grazing my cheek.

'Christ!'

He pulled my hand away to see the damage. 'It's okay, it doesn't bleed. You startled me.'

I tried to grin. 'Just as well the hammer was in your other hand.' Set against a throbbing skull, my stinging cheek was piddle. I stared at the block of stone. 'This all you got? I was expecting a quarry.'

'It's enough. When it's sold, I'll buy the next piece, that's how I work.'

'You got anything I can take? I'm hungover.'

He stroked the sullen granite. It might have been porcelain the way he laid his tools on top of it. 'Come.' Brushing past, he headed back into the box. The sun was warm. Following him, I shielded my eyes, afraid they'd shatter. He was pouring whiskey as I struggled in.

'Not that!'

'The hair of the lion. It's all I've got.'

My stomach mutinied. I brought the cup to my lips, trying to ignore the fumes, eyes watering as I fought for a while to hold it down.

'You drank more, last night. How come you don't feel it?' The floor was a churning sea as I braved it to the bench.

'You are smaller. Nor are you used to it.' He screwed the cap back on.

'Y'know, I've often wondered what your liver looks like? Anytime I've been to the bar with Mike, you're there. Must be a record.'

The alcohol burned in my throat and I began to feel its kick. My head lightened, even the throbbing became something I could handle. 'Why d'you drink so much?'

'Because I want. I don't use excuses.'

The whiskey was still doing its work. I felt careless.

'Well, I'd a hell of an excuse — isn't every day I find my lover groping another man.' I meant it to sound blasé, but somehow the words were drops of acid eating my guts all over again.

His eyes were careful. 'It was time you discovered.'

I stared. 'You knew? You knew Mike was ...? I mean, before I told you about it last night?'

His head jerked.

'Why didn't you tell me?'

He shrugged, shoulders lifting like branches. 'It wasn't my concern. I didn't know whether you knew and tolerated it. Finally, I don't know you well enough.'

'Terrific.' I wanted to spit. 'Dumb wife gets treated like a deaf-mute. I suppose Jan the Flagger knew it too? And Jacob?' I paused to catch breath, thinking of the others who frequented the bar, men who knew Mike, the same faces shooting pool every time we went there. How many of them had known? How many of them'd ...? The thought made me want to crawl under a rock.

'Except you're not his wife. In this respect, you're fortunate. He is a ... cruel man, he plays with people.'

'He's a shite.' The word gave me no satisfaction. I closed my eyes, trying to blot it out, hating myself when the question pushed through my lips. 'Have you seen him?'

'I heard he is living in Alkmaar.'

'Further the better.' But my voice carried no conviction. Despite what Mike'd done, I had no strength for hatred. Breathing itself was an effort. I'd even had to call in sick at the Institute, running the gamut of the principal's disapproval, the threats to divide my English classes between the other teachers and dismiss me 'forthwith' should my record of attendance slip below that which it had been 'heretofore,' — a crusty little gnome with a penchant for archaic phrases, renewing my contract annually to save paying me during vacations.

Suddenly I was squirming, afraid I'd wet myself. 'I need to go to the loo.'

He pointed to the curtain in the corner.

'You serious?'

'Ja.' He turned to look outside.

I hurried across. The coarse fabric hid a chemical toilet. I stepped behind the curtain, pulling it snug. But there was no refuge from sound, my zip the drone of an angry bee in the quiet. I closed my eyes against the image of him beyond, ears tuned. Squatting, I tried aiming the pee so it'd slide down the inside of the bowl. For the first time in my life I wished I had a penis.

When I emerged, my face was hot. I spoke quickly, out of a need to distract.

'So what's got you living in this thing? Must be freezing in winter.'

His back was a brick wall as he stared out through the bright opening. A couple of fields away, an ocean of young corn rippled, then stilled.

'Did you find it or what? Looks like it's ... lost, like it got shunted into some siding and forgotten.'

No answer. Had he heard? Lighting a cigarette, I stared at the rigid hawser of his neck. Well, he'd certainly heard me pee. Hadn't even the decency to step outside, let me do it in privacy. Sod him. 'I thought only little boys played with "chu-chus"?'

I might have struck him. He swivelled, eyes black slits of fury that made my skin bristle.

'Ja, you know what boys who play with trains grow up to be?'

I shrank as he strode across the boards, a dark silhouette carved from the outside day. What the hell had I spiked?

'They grow into men who play with numbers.' He paused, breath rasping the wood. I was afraid to say anything, sorry now I'd opened my mouth.

'Zo. You want to know why I live here, you want zi truth? I was seven years old when I had my first train ride. Lost, shunted into some siding, ja?'

He paused. I tried not to look at his fists, solid as cannonballs.

'When my mother complained it was a freight wagon the soldiers began to laugh. "Ja," they said. "Don't you know it yet, you lump of wood? Our cargo is oven-fodder." ' He stood, chest rearing as he sucked in air.

I couldn't grasp it. For something to do, I pushed the hair out of my eyes.

Suddenly, it connected: the tattooed number on his wrist I'd glimpsed in the bar: worn casually as a wristwatch, with neither the desire to conceal nor display. And the talk among those who knew his past. Sitting, I hunched over, chewing my bottom lip, not knowing what to say. An ant scurried past my sneaker, disappearing into a crack between the boards. How many cracks could the earth contain? I closed my eyes as the words hailed down.

'Numbers. Human digits. We were eighty-four. To be exact. In our wagon. At the start. When we arrived, we were sixty-seven. Eighty-four, take away sixty-seven —'

His voice got louder as he leaned over.

'Ja, these bodies ... these ... minuses ... you understand —?'

'Don't tell me!' I opened my eyes. It'd been a mistake to close them.

'Mostly the old, the ill. Seventeen over a distance of nine hundred kilometres. Average twenty box-cars to each train. The number of trains each day. The radius of countries from which they were consigned. In the meat of such statistics, a boy will acquire mathematical skills at a speed that would astonish you. But there's one kind of equation he never can master. Perhaps you know it? Perhaps you can say how these small boys grow up to play with trains?' He paused, finally. I breathed, hoping it was over. Outside, a bird prattled, defying the silence. But he wasn't finished.

'On the second day already there were two minuses. We stacked them in a corner, trying to keep a thin edge of space between us. Later, my mother stripped the chemise from one of them. For the rest of the journey, the adults took turns holding the cloth as a toilet screen in another corner.'

Jerking my head, I stared at the curtain. Jesus. 'You mean this, this is one —? No, don't tell me!'

'Ja, "don't tell me, I can pretend it never happened! I will not see what must not be!" Stomme! That's the attitude which drove us into those cars. That's how you lived with Mike!'

Dimly realising I'd moved, I found I was outside, hunkered on the blinding grass, my heart jigging. Damn the drunken impulse that'd drawn me here, he'd got to be crazy living like this, what was he, a bloody masochist, why had he wanted me to come back with him, why?

'You're shivering, we'll have something to eat, it'll warm you before you return to Zeist. Come.' His shadow blacked the grass about me but the calmness with which he spoke was steadying.

So. He was expecting me to leave. He didn't seem to have a plan to ... detain me. Yes, that was it, the word lurking in some dark hole in my mind since he'd hauled me on board. Opening my hands, I stared at the welts where the nails had bitten. The flesh stung in an odd way, as though it were something separate, something I could register, but couldn't feel. Like his pain.

I hesitated, watching him stride around the side of the box-car. As if in response, my stomach snorted, a loud, hungry eruption, making me wince. I hoped he didn't think it was a fart.

High above, against a slash of cloud, a kestrel hovered. What rustling contour had it fixed in its sights below on the mechanical map of polder and canal? What species of flesh, of, of ... animal fodder quickened the pulse of its instinct? A rabbit, limbs petrified as it sniffed the displaced air, heart speeding towards the hour of its extinction? For an instant I was both kestrel and prey, stomach snarling, heart scuttling as the bird swooped towards the horizon, cruelty in a blur of wings homing on fear.

'Komme!' The muffled word leaked through the wood. When I went round, he was squatting in the shade beside the granite, a plastic sheet set on the ground. I squinted at the food, swallowing a quick rush of saliva: cheese, bread, apples, white wine.

'Eat.' He poured the wine.

'Not here. Can't we go round front? I want to be in the sun.' A sudden breeze swept a layer of dust from the stone, misting its acute lines. 'I want to be in the sun.'

I couldn't see his face as he gathered the food.

'How d'you keep the wine so cool?' Walking beside him, I cradled the bottle, glad to find something ordinary to say.

'A safe in zi ground, I keep all the food there.'

'What about insects?'

He shrugged. 'It's sealed in a box.'

Sealed. I tried not to think. For a while we sat, eating in silence, the wine soaking my unease. By the time I'd finished, the regimental lines of the polders looked softer, less alien. I felt sure of myself again, foolish to've felt afraid. What harm could he do me, a man who haunted ghosts?

Lighting a cigarette, I tried to sound gentle. 'You shouldn't live ... in that thing, it, it isn't healthy, you can't go back.'

'Go back? You don't understand.' He poured the last of the wine, mouth twisting as he fought the words. 'I'm always ... on that train.'

'But you have to try and forget —'

His arm rose, sweeping my words aside. 'You're insane!'

What was calling me insane! Funny, almost. He flung the bottle. It wheeled in a wide arc towards the canal, clunking amidst squawks of protest.

'Forget? Never! You hear!'

I looked away. Meeting his eyes was like trying to outstare the sun.

'I am my past or I am nothing.'

'But what about the future? You've got to —'

'There's no future unless we face the presence of the past.'

'That's not what I meant —'

'Ja, but your question was puerile.'

Puerile. Terrific. He definitely had a way of making me feel wonderful. I closed my mouth to hide the way my teeth clamped. After a while I stretched, trying to make it look casual. 'Well, I'd better be going.'

No response. He drained his glass. I looked about for my anorak, then realised it was on the bed. Fuck it. I wasn't going back in there. I got up as he finally spoke. 'I can walk you back?'

'Really, there's no need.' All I wanted was to get away.

He stood, making me feel minuscule.

'Well, thanks, you know, the bed, and, and that.'

His lips thinned.

I tried not to hurry down the track in case he was watching. Suddenly the air was smashed by the clamour of iron on stone. I stopped dead. An elm near the canal erupted in a black swirl of flight.

I looked back. The pounding was relentless, dust steaming across the flat roof as though already it were nightfall, the mist closing in.

I was a bad choice, surely he could see it? I couldn't be the flesh among his spectres, I'd no room for his truth, the analytical way he made connections, just as I'd had no eyes for the hundred little warnings Mike had given.

I'd go back to my room, its neat grammatical lines, leave him here, haemorrhaging, a present participle I couldn't accommodate. As I couldn't accommodate what Mike had done. Yes, I'd go. Run from it. Now.

'I will not see what must not be.' The stone beat the rhythm of the words as he smashed it. I stood, the grass at my feet wavering in the breeze. Somewhere in it was the spider's web, its filigree trap bleeding through dawns and sunsets, the savage sameness of all the hours between.

Dragging back towards the box-car, I wished I were on some other planet, baring nothing save my skin to the blinding lick of a different sun. Oblivious.

Maeldúin of Africa

It's like I'm strapped inside this squealing pig as Uncle Bertie stops the lorry. When I climb down he gives me a pound note. 'You were a great girl for helping in the fields.' And he's gone. It's early, quieter than the country.

Crossing Sally's bridge, you can tell how hot it's going to be the way the sun's lying on the canal bed, a burst football stuck in the slime. I turn into the narrow terrace.

The boy from Africa's sitting on the footpath about half-way down, reading a book. Still here. Jesus. I squint over the plots at the canal shining but really I'm seeing him, legs spread out past the tar seams stitching the cracks on the road. Longer than Da's, though it's hard to tell what height Da is anymore, the way the drink makes his knees bend.

I pull my stomach in hard but the truth is I ate too much bread in Bertie's. How can someone I don't know make me feel like this? Least I'm clean, no smell of pee off my clothes because I haven't been stewing nappies this morning. That's about the only thing you can say in my favour. I wish Ma'd use bleach. I wish she'd stop having babies. I wish I'd never seen Da on top of her that night. I wish he'd go away someplace on a permanent binge. Nobody in this world should ever have to wipe up anyone else's vomit. Oh Ma. In the old photos, you look like a stranger in your own skin, someone I only know the look of. Beautiful. What happened you? I wish I looked like the photo-you, I wish I was beautiful. The boy is beautiful. And big. The closer I get, the bigger he seems, like he's growing in my mind with each step. My sandals're slapping the path in the quiet. I should've shaved my legs. The boy has no hairs on his legs or arms. Father Jack's brought him back from the

Missions. It's Father Jack's first holiday in eleven years and they're staying with his sisters, the Misses Moore. His name's Vusi. That's all Nora Donnelly managed to find out before I left for Uncle Bertie's.

When I get near, he lifts his head and our eyes crash. I look away quickly in case he thinks I fancy him.

'Did you have a nice holiday?' English, deep and clear. And speaking as if he knows me. I don't know what to do so I stop, lighting on the book.

'Hey, I have that one too.'

He points to my plastic bag. 'Your clothes?'

I nod, wishing I had a suitcase.

'Why don't you sit?' He slaps the footpath. 'Your mother won't be up yet.'

I hold the bag high to hide the way the bra makes me lumpy because it's too tight.

'Your mother always looks tired.'

For a stranger, he knows a lot. I put the bag down and sit on it. Air bursts out the top in a fart. I want to die. But all he does is laugh. His teeth're like my plastic pearls. His curls fit his head tight, like a swimming cap. My nose feels pinched when I look at his. He opens the book to inside the front cover and traces my name.

'Hey! It *is* my —!'

'Your mother lent it to me.' He flicks the pages. The matchstick girl I've drawn on the top right-hand corners begins to run. 'You've lots of books. The other kids here only seem to read magazines.'

I don't tell him the library man's given them to me because they're damaged.

'I didn't think you'd be staying this long.'

'We're going back tonight.'

'Back?'

'South Africa.'

'Oh!' I have this feeling inside of something dropping down fast.

He leans over with the book. I can smell the Sunlight soap Ma uses to wash the nappies before I boil them. He flicks the pages and there's this matchstick boy running up the book from the back.

'It's pencil, you can rub it out if you mind.'

But I don't. There's one page blank in the middle.

'I bet she gets there first,' I say.

'In Africa, they'd never meet. He'd live in a township and she'd be in the city.'

'I know about Apartheid.' I say it the way I've heard it on telly. For once I'm glad Ma makes me watch the news.

He tells me then he comes from a squatter camp outside a place called Guguletu. His father works in a factory cleaning chickens and they're saving for a concrete house with a tin roof. I can't get over him telling how poor he is. Ma always makes us say nothing when Da drinks the gas bill and we get cut off. Though we know everyone knows.

'Mr Mandela'll make things better ...' I say, '... y'know he's coming here soon?'

'A lot of us'll die before it gets better.' He says it like you'd say 'it's going to rain' when you know from the way the clouds're looking. The 'us' makes me shiver. I stare at the book. It's about this man Maeldúin who travels to piles of islands and has adventures. It's the one I always read when Ma stays in bed to hide the bruises.

'You must be Maeldúin, since you've come on a voyage to Ireland.'

'Comrade Father wants me to stay here with his sisters and finish school. My mother wants it too.'

Comrade. Sister Baptist'd say he was a Communist and that Father Jack was worse. He throws a stone. It flies over the waste plot and rips the water to shreds. While the ducks're going mad, something tightens inside me with the hope.

'And ... will you?' I manage it at last.

'No.'

One word and it's a door slamming in my face. 'There's too much to do at home, we have to fight for change. I'll go to school the day every black can vote.' His eyes're huge pennies staring at the sun, not even squinting. If Da could stare past Mooney's pub the same way, it wouldn't be so hard on Ma trying to keep me at school.

Before I'm old enough to vote I'll be in Manchester staying with Uncle Eric while I go to college, because I'll never get the points I need for here. Uncle Eric's promised, so long's Ma can pay my keep. Then later, with all the money I earn, I'll 've plenty to send to her. When Da's on a binge, that's what we talk about, that's our dream. But unless the ones who go away can find a way of coming back, we'll never vote here either. So nothing'll ever change. When I say this, he says that's why he has to fight, first to get the vote, then to use it to make everything fair and fuck school till then.

Across the canal the line of cars builds to a roar but the only reason I'm arguing is I hope he'll change his mind and stay. I can't believe I'm talking this much. And he talks like he's eaten his history, words like 'bloodshed' and 'democracy' and 'exile' and 'the struggle'. I can barely keep up. In the end I give up, he's got the same look in his eyes Da gets heading into Mooney's, and I know it's pointless.

'Why's it some patches of your skin 're blacker than others?' I blurt it because I don't want to think about him going back and what might happen.

'Why does your whole face go red sometimes?'

'It does not!' I stare down at the book.

'And why do I go red underneath the black?' He's grinning so much his jaws press his ears out of sight.

'You're crazy, how can a black person blush!' Suddenly I crack up and we laugh ourselves sick. His laugh rumbles so much it drowns out Ma's voice till I look up and see her waiting outside our house. The twins're dragging her dress fit to burst the seams but she doesn't notice. Her shoulders're sloping which means she's had more trouble with him. But even when I go in the scullery, she doesn't say anything, just talks and talks, filling me in on everything else, asking me questions about Bertie. I show her the vegetables in the bottom of the plastic sack.

'I'm glad you're home, Samantha's hopeless, you'd swear she was four instead a fourteen.' She squeezes the last of the nappies, damp triangles trailing from her armpits, isosceles, upside down, the apexes almost reaching the seam where her waist once was. It's her day off from the summer job. She's working in the bakery instead of me because I couldn't mix the dough quick enough. The pay's low but she won't complain, she's afraid the welfare aul' one'll suss her.

She's nodding at the vegetables. 'Did he give you anything else?'

I give her the money.

'Aul' skinflint got two weeks work out of you.' But she tucks it in the flap on the inside of her bra. 'Don't know what I'll do when we change to the coins, your Da'd hear a mouse farting feathers in the attic, just you remind me to leave it in with you.'

I hate wrapping her bra in my clothes at night so Da won't find the money. It's old and yellowed and the straps eat into her shoulders every time she's pregnant. Even the iodine can't hide how raw her skin gets. And through it all, she'll never say a word against him.

Later when the others call she makes me go out. 'I'll be back at work tomorrow and you won't get the chance.'

They're all talk outside. Vusi sits beside me on the path. I keep my head down in case he sees my face. I think he likes me. But if I can think that, he can think I like him too. It seems he's been everywhere with them, even fecking Ludlow's orchard.

'Vusi shook the trees so hard, the crabbers nearly brained us. The Bridge Stores took the lot, we made enough for all of us to go to the Savoy.' Tadghie Sweeney's grinning like I've never seen him since before his mother died. I try to smile, but I'm raging at what I've missed.

'Yeh, 'n we took him to the Hospice to see the dead bodies.' You can tell Linda Murray fancies him. It's in the brightness of her eyes and the way she keeps flicking her hair when she looks at him. She's lovely in the new jeans. I wrap my arms around my red knees jutting from the cut-offs. Even with jeans like that I'd never look like her. The good thing about having no illusions is you can never be disappointed.

It was Tadghie's idea to go to the Hospice, it's always his idea.

His Da wouldn't let him see his mother in the coffin, he'd the lid nailed down so fast Ma said it was a disgrace. Anyway, Tadghie saw on telly about people being sorry they'd never looked at the dead person, so he keeps going to the Hospice to see if he can find someone who looks like his Ma. I feel sorry for him but I wish he could stop searching; it makes me nervous.

'Well, y'didn't miss much up in Harold's Cross.' Nora Donnelly pokes me. She doesn't like seeing the bodies either.

'Ah, you two 're fecking cowards.' Tadghie walks over to the waste plot and pulls the weeds sticking through the fence. 'Death is a fact of life.'

'He heard that on telly, he doesn't believe in God y'know,' Linda tells Vusi.

'Holy Mary, fuck off, will you!' Tadghie's knuckles bleach better than the nappies. He cracks them over and over. Linda's face is puce and Nora nudges me.

I look at Vusi. 'Well, not many tourists get to see all the sights,' I say, hoping they'll laugh.

'I've seen much worse. When the police come into the townships ... people with their insides coming out ... once ... a woman with a baby sticking out of her stomach.' He says it low and flat and you wish he was lying. But it's the same way Tadghie talked when he told us his mother was dead and we didn't need to see her body either.

Tadghie stuffs the weeds in his mouth and gags. No one says anything. Ma's pregnant again. In a few months her stomach'll blow out, high and round, hard's a globe. The bra straps'll cut the grooves in her shoulders like a river.

'Ah c'mon, I've got a free gaff,' Tadghie says, wiping his mouth.

Round at his house, he puts on his tape of the 'Doors' but everyone groans so he stops the music. He starts talking about Jim Morrison, the lead singer. Who's dead. All Tadghie's favourite singers're dead. Nora turns on the telly while Tadghie pours a full glass of whiskey. 'Funeral whiskey,' he says. The news is on. He passes the glass, but Da's bleary eyes're enough to stop me tasting it. A bomb's gone off in a pub up the North and a soldier's hit a kid with a plastic bullet. Dead bodies again. Jesus. Tadghie pours cold tea into the whiskey bottle. Luckily his Da doesn't drink. The newsreader says it's Bloomsday. Nora says the whiskey tastes like wet turf.

'Boomsday?' says Vusi and everyone laughs.

'Yeh,' says Tadghie, 'y'know, the bomb in Belfast ... boom-boom ...' Already his face is flushed.

'Blooms,' Linda says, looking at her nails, 'flowers, y'know?' She smiles at Vusi. 'Probably the Flower Show in the RDS.' I open my mouth, then close it. Linda works evenings and weekends in Mooney's. It's not her fault she had to leave school. An old cowboy film comes on. Tadghie pours some sherry. 'Funeral sherry,' he says. In the film, the sheriff's counting cattle rustlers ... one-two-three ... as he shoots them. When he shoots the Indian tracker, he says 'eleven-and-a-half,' and we all laugh. Vusi jumps up, crashing past the sofa to get out of the room. The others think he's sick from the whiskey.

He's at Dolphin's Barn church before he slows down. I have to lean against the railings to get my breath.

'I'm ... sorry ... I'm really sorry!' But when I touch him he jerks away.

'You laughed with the rest of them!'

'I didn't think, really, I didn't —!'

'That's just the trouble!' His teeth knit like a zip. He turns his back and starts walking towards the terrace. In a few hours he'll go away from me.

'I'll never do it again!'

He stops and I smash into him. Across the canal the sun's sliding down the window of Scoil Íosagáin, our shadows locked in the glass bleeding onto the sill.

'Never!' I say.

He looks at me as if he's searching for something.

'Promise!'

'Honest ... I swear to God!' I say, though I don't believe. I don't know I'm crying 'till he reaches out and touches my cheek. Then he puts his finger to his lips and licks it. 'Salt ...' he whispers, '... the same as me ... remember?'

My throat pains so much I can't speak. Just as well he doesn't know about Ma buying the three black babies when she was at school.

We go into the waste plot past Hogans' potato drills because he wants to make some whistles for his sisters. While he's searching for reeds, I get stung by a wasp. I don't know what makes me scream, if it's the pain or Scoil Íosagáin's window getting bloodier. Vusi comes crashing up the bank and it's the first time I've seen him look afraid.

I'm crying again. 'A ... wasp,' I say, sounding a real whinge. Already my neck's swelling.

'The sting's still in it.' He makes me sit near the nettle-mountain and kneels beside me.

I twist so's he can see. He bends suddenly, putting his mouth over the sting. When he begins to suck, I bite my fist. He straightens, spitting into the nettles. Then he licks the pain, his tongue warm and wet against my skin. I get this queer feeling inside. After a while I can't feel the pain anymore, though I know it's there. Somewhere. It seems like we've made this space and only we are in it. There's no wind and no sound. The nettles're like statues, the canal quiet as glass. Even the sun's lukewarm to the heat inside. But I'll burst trying to bear it. I push him away. All I can hear's the way the two of us're breathing. He lifts a piece of my hair, lets it fall through his fingers. 'Like sand,' he says. When I touch his, it reminds me of poodle wool. If I can get the guts to lift my head, he'll kiss me. But just then we hear the others rip-roaring as they climb into the plots.

Before he leaves, I squeeze the money out of Ma to buy him the pen in the Bridge Stores. It has 'Souvenir of Dublin' on it, with a little black shamrock for a full stop. I like the shamrock being black. There's hardly time to push it into his hand before the priest's car from Adam and Eve's takes them away. The street's queer and empty even though everyone's around.

When I go in, Ma and Da're standing in the scullery, arms around each other, crying. No knowing what the truth of them is.

But not knowing doesn't stop me being afraid some morning I'll find the truth of her on the scullery floor, her eyes blanked out, a half-made baby's grave deep in the mound of her stomach. Boom.

Later, when he's gone drinking, we watch the news. More about the North. The kid would've been eleven tomorrow. Two girls in the pub toilet when the wall collapsed, a lipstick in one of their hands. Thirteen dead in South Africa. Boom-boom. Ten hours before he lands on the other side of the globe, before I start having to search for the truth of him, just like Tadghie searches.

I'm glad to go to bed. My Maeldúin of Africa. There's a country in my head where we're walking on a beach of fine sand, where all kinds of people 're allowed to be together. When Vusi kisses me, I taste the salt on his lips like a tear. Thinking each detail makes the picture seem real as truth, so that then I know all the while I'm growing up and growing old, whenever I stand on a beach somewhere, by the edge of the sea, I'll remember Vusi's kiss.

Downstairs, Da's come in. Soon the rowing begins. Boom. I stuff the blanket in my mouth and scream.

East of Ireland

It's two weeks since I heard, yet still I am confounded by it. Hans doesn't know. But I must tell him soon. I delay only because I know what his reaction will be.

'Get rid of it,' he'll say, in the same tone he uses every time there's a mess. Like that time he used a spade on the beech marten which had nested in the attic, causing us longer nights.

Today is market day in Alkmaar and I have come to shop among the stalls. For the first time, Rhein of the cheeses can't tempt me with the subtleties of taste between the ageing Goudas. Although it's spring, the tourists haven't yet descended for the ritual parading of produce before the stalls burst into action.

I have bought raw herring for Hans. Pickled in brine. In the glass it floats, dead and grey. Like a foetus. It is in this moment standing at the fish stall that I decide: this moment when my eye wanders from the herring to the eels burrowing in the crushed ice; I will tell him tonight. I watch the fishmonger select a sinewy black body from the marble slab and hold it out like a ruler to the woman before him.

'Nice. Will it feed three of us, do you think?' she asks him in Dutch. It twists, sunlight glancing off the glistening skin.

'Ja, seker. He is good and fat.' The man holds the knife poised. At a nod from the woman, he sets to work. As he scrapes the neatly cut pieces into the plastic bag, they are still writhing.

When I return to the house, Hans is above in his studio. I listen at the foot of the stairs. Unable to hear the scrape of his palette knife, I am unsure whether to be pleased by the silence. Sometimes it can mean he's working: but sometimes it means he's staring out at the lake. When he's spent hours like this, he'll always come down in a black mood, but he'll never tell me why. Still, it's better than the noise, for when his painting is going badly, he breaks things and his furious pacing rams the kitchen ceiling, sending flakes of whitewash snowing to the floor.

For no reason I can fathom, except perhaps the drive home past flower-fields stretching their rainbows to the horizon, I am hopeful. In the garden, the crocuses are burgeoning. I want to take some, set their sweet insistence in an eggcup on the table. But if I do, he'll frown at my frivolity. 'You've butchered them,' he'll say, as he once said when I cut some daffodils. That's something about him I have grown used to: he'll always repeat words without a single deviation from the way he strung them together the first time. Knowing this, I'm never inclined to make the same mistake twice. But tonight there'll be new words: a new frame of reference. Despite my hopefulness, I am afraid.

———

He has come down, his presence filling the air so that the walls have shifted, closed in tightly. By the time he had come, the sun had already deserted this old high-ceilinged kitchen. But the snap of the lightswitch was not enough to dispel the shadows.

I told him then, the words tumbling in a torrent as I served the food. He said nothing. He sat and ate.

Unable to bear it, I pushed my plate of food aside. 'What d'you think?'

'I think nothing.' He swirled the wine in his glass, his eyes watchful under hooded lids, a cat in a cage waiting for a child to stretch its hand between the bars.

I waited. It was only when his English slipped a little that I could decipher it. But still he didn't speak.

'You must think something. It's a child —'

His hand slammed the table and the glass spun, wine spilling blood across the light oak.

'It's a thing. A parasite. Feeding on you. I will tell you something.' He turned to look at me, the words erupting from the hard rim of his mouth. 'It will not feed on me.'

In the silence, the drip from the tap pounded the cracked enamel.

'You have heard me, yes?'

I managed a nod.

'When you get rid of it, I will have a vasectomy. This stupidity will not happen again.'

'Stupidity. That's all it is to you.'

'It was stupid to become impregnated.'

'You make me sound like a cow. Like you'd nothing to do with it.'

'You were supposed to control it.'

'For God's sake, Hans, I couldn't take the pills. That time when I was sick —'

'You should have taken them.'

'I couldn't. Doctor Bon made me stop while he gave me the injections. And you ... you still wanted —' I was bitter, remembering.

'You should have told me.'

'I forgot. I forgot. How can you expect me to remember things like that when I'm sick?'

He leaned forward. 'When do you get rid of it?'

'I ... I didn't arrange anything.' I gulped some wine.

'No!'

The word thudded in my ear. He stood abruptly, his chair overturning to crack on the tiles.

'If that's what you want, you must leave. I made it clear to you from the first. I want no children. You agreed.' He began pacing, his shadow lashing the walls.

'I want to have it.' I didn't think he heard above the staccato of his steps. But he stopped suddenly.

'Then go.'

'Where? Where can I go? I've no money, nothing. Please.' I turned to him. 'Don't make me —'

'It's your choice. I wash my hands. I'll give you some money. You can go back.'

I stood, screaming. 'You know I can't go back, you know it. Don't say that to me.'

'Then stay. Get rid of it.' He jerked a bottle from the wine rack and began to open it, swearing as the cork split.

I was shaking. Once before he'd been this cruel. He'd gone to Ireland, tried to force me to go with him. But I couldn't go back. I'd waited a long time for him to return, but when he did, he wouldn't speak to me for the first ten days, he was in such a black sulk. Then he said, 'It's primitive, your country, full of bleak landscapes. Never have I seen so many tones of grey. I painted much.' He talked of when the crates of his paintings might arrive and when I had begun to relax, he said it. 'The house of your father is beautiful. Not at all the gothic horror you described.'

I waited, afraid. But he was better at such games than I. When I could bear it no longer, I asked him, almost gagging on the words. 'What did you do?'

He shrugged, but his eyes were alert. 'It seemed a pity to pass it. I was interested in its architecture, those Ionic columns.'

'Liar.'

He ignored me. 'I called one day. Your father was kind enough to let me sketch it.'

'Liar. You're lying.'

'I'll show you the sketch when it arrives. Done from inside the grounds —'

'I don't want to see it. You bastard. How dare you! I told you to stay away.'

'Have you no wish to know how your parents are? What we talked of?'

'Fuck, fuck you for doing this!' I had run and locked myself in the cellar. Hours later I came out. But only when he'd promised me that he'd said nothing to my parents about me, about where I was, and that he'd never speak of it, never taunt me with it again.

Now, as he handed me a glass of wine, he repeated it, 'Get rid of it.'

The words drummed in my head, keeping time with the tap. I drained the glass, the lightness filling me with courage. 'I want to stay. And I want to have it. You'll feel different about ... Once it's born ...' I hiccuped, my voice caving, losing its conviction.

'Listen to me.' He sat close, grasping my shoulders, his skin laced with the smell of white spirit. 'I don't want it, you understand?'

'But why? For God's sake tell me —'

'This world is a sick place. I won't subject anyone else to it. Nor will I be tied to it any more than I can help.'

'Then you might as well be dead.'

'Precisely what I strive for. To be dead alive. To feel nothing.'

'What about me?'

'You, ja, I've told you, often. But with no excess baggage.'

'Sometimes we've been happy. Haven't we been —'

He laughed, the sound beating my face.

'We're a lie. For those who face reality, there is no happiness. Look to you. You have run away from what you could not face. You hide here with me —'

'And you? What great truths d'you face? You're hiding too.' I winced as his grip tightened.

'You stupid bitch. Listen to me. I hide from nothing. Nothing, you understand?' He jumped up and I shrank as he raised his hand. When the blow didn't come, I opened my eyes. He was standing at the window, staring through the blackness towards the lake.

I watched the rigid trunk of his back, his roughened hands gripping the edge of the sink as though he would wrench it apart.

'This time only, I'll speak of it. Then again, never. You will not interrupt. When I have finished, you will not interrogate me.'

I stared at him. I never knew what to expect. Everything came in spurts from him, his anger, his need of me, his sudden obsessions with work. Even in his hair there was nothing uniform, no blending of colours. Instead, streaks of white slashed the black as effectively as paint.

'Now, listen to it,' he snapped.

'My home was Bruckhausen, a small village on the East German border. The war was almost over. We were old men, children and the women. The young men were away fighting. All the German forces east of Danzig isolated. The Russians were in Poland. We lived on rumours of the continuing advance of General Zhukov's armoured columns. One day word came that they had been sighted crossing the Brandenburg frontier. The next we heard that one of Zhukov's spearheads had reached the lower Oder near Kustrin.

'We were all of us, trapped.

'We ran to the church. The children were bundled to a corner. The adults talked. Later, my grandmother told me how it was decided. The thaw had already set in on the Oder, and the next morning at first light the people would go together to the river: to drown. The strongest among us would help those weak, hold the children under.'

He swung around suddenly and stared. Had I spoken? I didn't know.

'You must understand what it was for us. These Russians, we'd killed three million of them, ja? They hated us deeply the same as we hated the Jews.'

Striding to the table, he poured some wine. The bottle knocked erratically against the glass. And his eyes. Black with it. I didn't want to hear any more. But I was afraid to move. While he drank, I filled my own glass. In the silence, the tap reasserted itself, racing towards some horror I didn't want to grasp.

'I had twelve years then. Tall for my age. Greater than my grandmother.' He paused, his raucous tone filling the room. 'Oma made me promise when we got to the river, I would hold her under.' He turned abruptly and flung his glass at the window. 'I kept it!' The words were a hoarse roar above the shattering glass. When I opened my eyes his face was bleeding from several cuts. I tried to get up, but it was as if I had no legs.

'You've cut —'

'Listen!' His face contorted. He wiped a small dribble of blood that hovered on his eyebrow, streaking it across his forehead.

'When we reached the river, the Russians were already there, flanking the east bank. There were two divisions, the first on horseback. Behind them the heavy Stalin tanks of the infantry. Already people had begun jumping into the river. There was much screaming as the Russians drove their horses into the water. The current was swift with the pull of the Baltic thirty kilometres north. Some were swept downstream before the Russians could reach them. Others struggled with the soldiers and were stunned in the thrashing hooves of the horses. Many were drowned.

'Oma never struggled. Not even when ... When I was sure it was done, I plunged into the mainstream, for swimming with the current. Suddenly I was seized on the collar, being pulled towards the east bank. I could not get at the rider. Even I kicked at his horse. It made no difference. That Russian bastard saved me.' He ground glass underfoot. A cold wind ruffling his hair, carrying the strong briny tang of the lake into the room. Beyond the broken window, the clouds glowed with the faint rumour of moonlight.

'On the bank, there were many others that the Russians had pulled out.'

'What happened?'

'Nothing! Nothing happened! All. All of it.' The words tore at the air. 'For nothing. The Russians never harmed one of us. They had only seventy kilometres from Berlin. They were too busy on getting there, too busy to kill us. They continued to advance southwest, leaving a small garrison in the village.'

'It wasn't your fault.' I was sorry as soon as I'd spoken. He hated sympathy.

'Stupid! There is no blame to apportion. Except, perhaps the superstitions, the fears, of the old. And my mother. The sow who bore me. She and several of the younger women hid in the church. Afraid to come to the river. Several days later, the bodies floated, some of them trapped in the thick bushes far down the bank: others snagged in the rocks of ice that had not yet thawed, their faces and bodies half eaten away. And the smell —. When you breathed in, it stayed inside you.' His shoulder shook as he unfurled his hands, staring down at them. 'Oma was not among them.' He came to the table, splashing more wine into a glass.

'By now, my mother was whoring with a Russian officer. I ran away. Our soldiers had launched a counter-defensive against the Russians on the Neisse. After three weeks of sneaking and crawling through the countryside, I managed to join them. They laughed at how crazy I was to fight. Nevertheless, they gave me a gun. But within weeks, the Russians burst from their bridgeheads across the river. We were defeated. Many of us were captured. I was ten years in one of their ... wonderful camps.'

I stared at him as he crossed to the wine rack, splinters of glass snapping on the tiles. I thought of those people he painted, their faces like cold, dead fish, my own among them. I saw then all it could ever be was this, cold and dead inside me, floating in its amniotic brine. I had no courage for it to be otherwise.

'Salut!' he said harshly and raised the bottle, drinking half its contents before he lowered it.

I dragged myself from the chair and began to push the brush about the floor.

'Leave it. Come upstairs.'

'You didn't have to break it. You didn't have to. You didn't.' I heard the glass rattling and scraping under the brush, but I couldn't see it, everything was blurred. I knew then I was crying but I couldn't feel it, I could only feel what he'd done.

'It was necessary. You wanted me to tell you. Now you must decide.'

But it was already done. He had seen to that. 'It's a mess. All a mess.'

'Come.' He took the brush from me.

'It'll be a mess. A terrible, terrible mess. Half-fleshed, like your bodies. And bones?' I looked up at him as he led me toward the door. 'Will there be bones?'

'How many weeks gestation have you?'

I wrenched myself from him, screaming. 'I'm not an animal, it's not an animal!'

'That's precisely what it is, what we are. What other animal treats its own kind as —? We're not even animals. We're savages.'

'Fuck you! Just leave me alone.'

'Very well. Nevertheless, you must remember. If you give that thing a life it will become oppressor or victim. A wonderful choice for it, ja?' He strode to the door.

'What about me!'

'What of you?' He turned. 'You will be the sow who bore it.' The door crashed behind him.

——————

I sit at the table, my head laid in the wood. 'Too busy to kill.' And Hans? Too full of it to live. I stay for a long while, hating him, picturing how it will be. Pieces of eel writhing in the sac: scraped away like his knife across the wooden palette. Every day he paints I'll listen for it, just as every day he watches the lake.

It's still dark. Yet through the window comes the first stirring of the waterfowl, the widgeons, teal and mallard that nest in the sedge along the banks. Though it's not yet winter, I remember the goosander he once freed from the ice, carrying it into the house, his hands torn from the saw-toothed edges of its bill. He was a long time fitting the splint on its forewing; the sleek feathers an iridiscent quiver under his touch; the bird's frantic whistles piercing the grimness in his eyes.

Later, nearer summer, we stood watching its awkward run to take wing from the garden. And his face. Losing some of its austerity.

The icy coldness drives me upstairs. He's awake, waiting in the dark, the window bare.

'I'll call Doctor Bon in the morning.' I'm shivering.

'Optimal,' he says, rubbing my back. But the cold is inside me.

'No more raw herring.'

'Whatever.' He rubs my skin more vigorously as we lie staring among the phosphorescent shadows the moonlit water casts about the walls of the room.

The Lost

Four a.m. and she still hadn't returned. He began to sweat. Despite this, for something to do, he kept banking the fire 'till the chimney roared with protest. Outside was freezing night, every glazed branch, every bush transfixed under a sky frosted with stars, the sudden descent of Siberian weather holding a startled Dublin in thrall.

And Maria was out in it, slip-sliding her way over pavements of cobbled ice as she combed the warren of streets making up the city. Her eyes, Feilim knew, devouring as she searched among the faces for a sign, some clue.

One of these nights she'd get herself killed, she wouldn't return. This was neither a new, nor a frightening thought, but tonight for some reason it made him shiver. He poured another drink, the sizzle of whiskey on ice momentarily blotting out the persistence of the mantel clock.

Tock, he decided as he began pacing the long living room, must be the past of tick. Tick-tock now-past tick-past now-tock tick-gone tick-gone tick-on. Click, went his heels pacing the polished boards, click-tock, tick-clock, louder now, pacing towards the only certainty for both of them ever since the child had disappeared.

Which object in the attic had upset Maria tonight, driven her out into the freak Siberian streets? One of the toys, most likely, it'd been a long time since she'd last tried to set the cot alight. Well, whichever thing it was, let her not have taken the axe to it or he'd have a terrible job putting the pieces back together. He should have hidden the axe after what she'd done to the jack-in-the-box, why hadn't he hidden it? Why? Why? The question began to infuriate him as he paced. Spilling his drink a little down the front of his business suit, he hurried from the room and took the winding stairs two at a time till he reached the little attic room with the dormer window overlooking the park.

But she'd used the hand-saw on the donkey, the huge, shaggy turquoise brute he'd won at the rifle range when they were honey-mooning in Spain, when the child was already seeded in her.

'Why, you can put rockers on it, it'll make a grand rocking ass,' she'd said, laughing, running her fingers through its silky blond mane. And he'd finally done so, for the child's fourth Christmas.

Now the straw entrails oozed from the slit belly and throat and the donkey leaned drunkenly against the cot, gazing cross-eyed at him, its shocking pink lips puckered in apology. Feilim pushed the straw back in, took the donkey downstairs and sewed it up with the nylon thread strong as cat-gut he kept for just such purposes.

He grimaced at his handiwork as he drained the whiskey bottle. An ass with a huge idiotic grin. A thin strand of mane had got sewn in the neck slit, and he snipped it close to the line of sutures, the strand rasping under the blade. It might have been hair. Maria carried a tendril of hair in the locket about her throat. Blond as the donkey's mane, blond as his second mistress's, blond as Lulu's Nordic swathes next door. Lulu, now what was it about Lulu? Yes, fuck, fuck it, he had forgotten to check on her, Christ. He hurried out into the frozen garden, the whiskey pulsing in his blood-stream as the stars reeled beyond the skeletal branches and his breath smoked on the icy air.

But when he looked up at the house next door, all was darkness and peace, when his gaze tracked the cypresses to Lulu's balcony, no tricolour was tied to the glistening railings, all he could see was a patch of icy sky flickering behind bars. Lulu was safe, the lout she was married to was either on the wagon, or so inebriated that he didn't have the energy to raise a hand against her tonight. Or he was dead. Feilim grinned. They all should be so lucky.

While he was standing thus on the gravel, the cold eating through the thin fabric of his suit, the sound of a truck labouring into the street suddenly pierced the stillness. Maria, he thought, as he withdrew into the slippery porch and stood listening to the groans of the approaching engine. Maria. Only her return could

account for the amount of horse-power advancing down the gen-
teel, suburban street. When it turned into the drive, he saw the dark
mountain of clay it carried, the duffle-coated men leaning on their
spades as they took a break from the monotonous task of gritting
the streets to loosen the stranglehold of ice.

Leaving the hall door ajar, Feilim moved back into the living
room and stood shivering, his back to the dying fire. He heard the
voices outside above the roar of the engine, the sudden raucous
laughter of one of the men. He heard Maria call her thanks to the
driver, her apology for taking him out of his way. He heard the
driver capitulate when she pressed him to take the money. The
boards under Feilim shuddered as the lorry set off back down the
drive. When he finally heard the footsteps crossing the hall, they
told him nothing new, nothing beyond the fact that Maria had yet
again found someone, had brought that someone back.

But as he stood facing the open door, a small, fat duck waddled
in, snowy-white, with a deep yellow bill. Fixing its eye on the
grinning donkey, it gave a ferocious squawk that sent a shock of
feathers rippling from its sleek neck to its tight little duck-ass. Its
head reared, every alert feather on the offensive. Feilim stared,
open-mouthed. Almost five a.m., and a furious duck stood quivering in his living-room. 'A drowning fuck,' he said, the whiskey
winning the war between articulation, logic and incredulity. He
stood bemused as the duck shot forward to assault the shaggy,
synthetic leg of the donkey.

'It belongs to Lady,' Maria said as she entered. 'This is Lady.'
She drew a diminutive old woman, glazed-eyed and toothless, into
the room, and the air suddenly thickened. Even from where he
stood, Feilim got the whiff of stale sweat and piss from the shabby
coat, and, overriding it, the scent of Maria's perfume. She must
have doused the old woman in it.

'How do you do?' said Feilim mildly.

The old woman peered at him warily, then nodded. 'The Pre-
shident got shtuck to the canal, couldn't move one way or d'other,
glued sholid to the ice, could've froze to death, she could, if it washn't
for the Mischsus here.' A bony hand clutched Maria's wrist.

'The President, oh yes?' Feilim inquired politely, trying to sound as if he understood.

'Wash her feet,' said the old woman from a wealth of rubbery gums, 'wash her feet, the webbin' got shtuck d'y'shee now?'

Feilim didn't. But he nodded anyway as she clutched a gin bottle and a brown paper parcel to her bird breasts.

'The duck's name,' said Maria, looking at him doe-eyed, 'is Mary Robinson.' Feilim felt the knot of tension in his gut ease as he registered the blandness in her face. She was back.

Pawn to king four, he thought, proceed with caution. 'I fixed it,' he said, nodding at the donkey, keeping his own expression equally bland. If all her anger had evaporated, she would ignore what he said.

'Bath-time,' she said to the old woman, 'Mrs Robinson needs a bath to remind her what the canal's like when it's thawed.' Feilim turned away in relief.

The duck squawked with fury as the women prised her loose from the shaggy leg of the donkey.

'Shure she's driven dishtracted be the colour of the assh, she ish, though it'sh the besht-looking duck-egg assh I ever sheen,' said Lady, stroking the donkey while Maria prised a tuft of turquoise from the vice-grip of the yellow bill.

When they went upstairs, Feilim wiped up the duck-shit. All over the house the pipes suddenly clanked and hammered as water was disgorged into the old bathtub on the first landing.

Feilim grinned. It wasn't just Mrs Robinson who was in for a soaking. For the old woman, the next hour would add new meaning to the act of having a bath with your duck. Of all the battles with all the people Maria had dragged back to the house over the years, this was one she had never yet lost.

Feilim made tea while he waited, and packed the cookie jar with plain digestives so the old woman could dunk them. He had wheeled the trolley through to the living room and was pouring the tea when the women returned.

Still clutching her parcel, the old woman flapped across the boards, her sparrow-frame lost in the silken folds of Maria's pink pyjamas, her downy wisps of hair, which Feilim had thought to be grey, turning out to be as snowy as her duck's.

Her eyes popped as she saw Feilim open a fresh bottle of whiskey and lace the tea with it. 'Well, man-dear! Be shure now,' she said as she sat on the donkey, 'that y'give ush a good big mug a that shtuff to flush out me bones, yer Mishush here'sh a bit too fond a water for me liking, ah never mind them thingsh now!' Reaching for the mug, she waved aside the biscuits Feilim proffered.

'Where's the duck?' Feilim handed Maria a mug, his gaze skidding away from the little hairbrush in her hand.

'Thish ish the mosht beautiful assh I ever sheen the like a,' said Lady, stroking the silky strands of the mane as the donkey rocked slowly back and forth under her skeletal grip.

'Where's the duck?' Feilim said again.

Maria set her mug down, the tea untouched as she watched the moving donkey. 'She wouldn't come out of the shower,' she said absently. Moving to the old woman, she began to stroke the brush through the downy hair. Feilim stared, mesmerised. Without lifting his gaze from Maria's hands, he took a swig from the whiskey bottle and moved to sit by the hearth. 'Oh yes?' he said, unaware he was raking the warm yellow ash in the grate. Sparks flew like chaotic stars. He wouldn't go into work today; Collins could oversee things for him on the Four Courts job.

'We left it running on her. She's standing there under the shower, her head tucked under her wing, she's sleeping, isn't she, Lady?' Maria's eyes were dreamy.

The old woman drained her mug and set it down on the boards. 'She thinksh itsh raining she doesh, the eejit,' she said, opening her parcel and taking out an ancient black telephone.

'You can stay as long as you want, the two of you, isn't that so, Feilim?' Maria said, without looking at him.

Lady began to dial a number.

'As long as you want,' said Feilim gruffly as he watched.

'Ish that yerself, Mattie?' Lady whispered into the receiver and paused, listening.

Maria pressed the child's hairbrush to her cheek. 'Forever, if you want,' she said.

'Not a bad place at all, in outta the cold anyhow with the besht-looking assh y'ever sheen.' Lady grinned, her gums reaching back to her ears.

'Isn't that so, Feilim?' said Maria.

'That's right, Mattie, me own shining shteed!' Lady laughed long and hard, blasts of soured breath spicing the air.

'Look,' whispered Maria, opening the locket and gazing at the lock of hair. 'One day, a Tuesday, the sun was splitting ... he never came home from school ... He's been lost for years, isn't that so, Feilim?'

When Feilim stayed silent, Maria pressed the locket to her breasts. 'Splitting deep.' She placed a hand on Lady's knobbly shoulder. 'Feilim doesn't believe he's still alive, you see.'

'Shure I'll give yeh a ring sho again tomorrow.' Lady hung up abruptly and climbed off the donkey. 'Maybe now,' she said, picking up her mug as she looked across at Feilim, 'yeh'd give ush another shup a yer holy water?'

Feilim rose, handing her the bottle.

'Well, blessh yeh, man-dear,' said Lady, as she added more whiskey to the teapot.

Feilim moved to Maria and closed the locket before his gaze could fall on the hair.

'The colour of Feilim's second mistress's,' Maria said, still looking at the locket, and he strained to remember whether the thought had first been hers or his own, so deeply embedded in each of them now was the need to be surrogate for the other.

Maria picked up the telephone from where Lady had placed it on the donkey's back. In the chrome dialling wheel, Feilim caught a glimpse of two minuscule faces trapped between the finger-holes.

'Manna,' said Lady, dribbling a little as she poured the tea-stained whiskey.

'Hello ...' Maria whispered into the dead receiver, her wide gaze anxious as she tracked some inner space. 'Hello ... hello ...?' Then she pressed it against Feilim's ear and searched his face as she waited. But placing his hand over hers, Feilim gently returned the receiver to its cradle, afraid he too would hear what she heard every breath, day and night, year in, year out.

The Edge

I was a year back in Los Angeles when I ran into my stepfather at one of Lucy's parties. I hadn't seen him in five years. He hadn't come to my mother's funeral, though it wasn't the cost of the fare to Ireland that stopped him. I pictured the god-forsaken cemetery where she was buried, the bleak lake below it, and hated the tanned healthy cut of him. He was standing in a corner talking to the kind of women he liked. Fragile, like polished shells. Like my mother.

'Didn't know. Sorry,' Lucy hissed.

'Who brought him?' I turned my back to rearrange my face.

'Dunno. Jack Waldhorn? They're doing a lot of business together lately.'

He came over, drink in hand. Lucy sheered away like a frightened rabbit. Some pal.

'Well, look what the cat dragged in,' I said.

'Hello bitch,' he said, the tic above his jaw racing.

'Gee, Pops, what a way to greet your little gal.' I watched the colour spread upwards into the silver streaks of hair. Dyed? They were too good-looking to be natural.

'I believe your lovers have all been my age?' He held out the glass.

I needed it. Yet I couldn't take it. He'd see my nervousness.

'I'm careful who I drink with. Not quite your age, actually. When I was eleven, you were forty-one. Already an old man. A dirty, dirty old man.'

'Crap. You were old as the hills when I married Leda. Eighteen, going on eighty.'

I was jealous of my mother's name on his lips. 'You know what I mean!' My words swelled in the roar of conversation, checking its flow. Several heads turned to stare under the blaze of lights. His fingers cut into my arm, pulling me towards the balcony.

'I've had enough of your scenes to last me a lifetime.' Outside, the night was finally cooling. The party sounds muted as he slid the glass door shut. I wasn't scared. No matter how far I'd gone, he'd never hit me. I grabbed the drink he was holding and drained it.

'Dutch courage?'

I dropped the glass into a tub sprouting an orange tree. Several leaves were black, in the grip of some necrosis. 'There's a bad taste in my mouth,' I said, meaning him.

'Was there much pain? When she?'

The suddenness of it left me winded. I walked to the rail, needing its support. Below, the lights on the highway hurtled like chaotic stars.

'Not near what you put her through.'

'Did she ... mention me?'

I stared up at the black sky. Unfathomable. Like her face.

'Don't flatter yourself.' But I was lying. She died with his name in her eyes. Not mine.

I turned, throwing back my head. Even in stilettos, I felt like a midget next to him. But I needed to look him in the eyes. 'I wish you'd died. Instead of her.'

'Well, tough shit, honey.' He loosened his tie. A sign he was upset. 'You shouldda been the one. That time you took those pills after I married her. Wouldda solved all our problems. I'd a never had to leave her.'

Sweat tickled the hollow between my breasts. 'She died because you left.'

'Don't try pinning it on me. She died because of the cancer.' He must have done some nosing to find that out.

"Sides, I didn't leave her. I never left her. I left you.' The words were flung in my face.

I was silent, wondering what he meant. Through the plate glass I watched people jerking, grinning. Stringed puppets, the warm lights softening their outlines. It seemed like we'd been shoved out

on the rim of the world to watch a movie with the sound turned
down. Suddenly, I was afraid I'd never get back in. 'I'm going.'

'Noplace. Not till you hear a few home truths.' He moved,
blotting out the giant screen.

'Then you'd better be willing to face a few yourself.'

'I never laid a hand on you.'

'Everytime you looked at me, it was there.'

'It was your fault. Going around half-naked, like there was no
man in the house.'

I couldn't resist it. 'There was no man.'

'I'm a little old to be sidetracked by that shit. You planned it all
to get rid of me. When you couldn't grab her attention with the fake
suicide, you started in on me.'

'Really? And I suppose I planned it so's you'd come to my room
that night?'

'I never touched you.'

'Not with your hands, no.' I drawled the words deliberately,
making him remember how he'd stood there, the heat in his face
as he'd watched me.

'I was tight. I wasn't going to —'

'To?'

'Do anything you didn't want. Babe.' Getting his own back,
letting me know he knew.

If only I hadn't wanted it. But I had. Then Leda walked in and I
reached for the robe, trying to hide it; unable to bear her startled
face. Like a child being punished for no reason it can fathom. That
was when my mother became my child.

'I could forgive you if it weren't for that night. Making her doubt.
She never trusted me again, you bitch.'

'I said nothing.'

'That was the trouble. The two of you, all cosy, shutting me out.'

I shrugged, trying to look calm. 'Why rake it —?'

'By the time I had it figured, she was dying.'

In the dark, I caught a snarl of teeth as he watched.

'I'm going in.' I made to pass him but he pushed me back.

'I'd a never noticed if you'd a covered yourself properly.' He moved closer, whiskey on his breath. 'But you wanted me, you little tart. To get at her.' He paused, and I heard it coming in the sudden staccato of his breathing. 'Maybe it's time.'

My skin bristled. 'Time?' I said. But the question was merely a decoy.

'Yeah, time you paid.' The words sprang from his mouth. He waited, the whites of his eyes glittering as he peered closer. Too vain to wear his glasses.

'Okay, then. I'll pay.' I said it quietly to keep my voice steady.

He wasn't expecting it. It took him awhile, working his mouth to form some words. 'Brazen as ever.'

'You want to or no?' I couldn't believe my ears. It sounded like I'd asked if he wanted a smoke.

He stood staring. The air was cooler now, an excuse for the way I was shivering.

'Fuck you!' He reached suddenly, gripping my shoulder, propelling me towards the glass.

Afterwards I often thought how if I'd planned it, it'd never have happened. I think it was the same for him, but I can't be sure. There was a small room at the end of the hall, a room that Lucy used for storing things. No air-conditioning. The biggest thing it stored was the heat, the air swarming over us when he opened the door.

There was a narrow bed but we didn't use it.

He wouldn't let me switch out the light or close my eyes. He hurt me as much as he could and I welcomed it. It made me able to live with the lies I'd told her. Made it all true.

But he was wrong. About why I had done it. I'd wanted a father yet when Leda brought him home I knew it couldn't be like that. I wanted them both. In the evenings I'd watch them together on the couch, heads close, absorbed in old photos under the arc of lamplight I'd once shared with her. From the shadowy edge of that arc, I watched.

When he slid from me, I waited for the relief. But there was none. Dressing was painful. Unlocking the door, I glanced down. He lay, eyes closed. Crying.

Staggering down the hall, a spurt of semen soaked the cotton crotch of my underpants. I stopped, expecting eyes to stare accusingly from the noisy lighted doorways. Nothing happened.

Outside, the sky was still black, the smog obliterating the stars.

It was ten years and six towns later before the letter from his lawyer caught up with me. I'd heard he'd died. Lucy and her sporadic postcards. The lawyer enclosed a letter from him, written a couple of days before his death. My name was typed on the outside, the print identical to the lawyer's letter. Inside, a single sheet, thin as skin. 'Goodbye bitch,' it said, his handwriting a scrawl I barely deciphered. I wondered what the lawyer thought.

While I sat staring at it, the boy walked into the room. Nothing of me is evident in him. What is in me gnaws like the canker on the orange leaves. I speak sharply and instantly his wounded eyes are Leda's. But the hard line of his mouth is my stepfather's. So I cannot escape. Even sweating and heaving with other men under black ceilings, I am always on the edge of it.

The Road to Austerlitz

His voice rammed the wood as I stood outside, shivering in the dark. He was worked up, otherwise he wouldn't have used my name. I didn't get time to answer.

'Where were you?' The door strained on its hinges as he flung it wide.

'In the woods.'

'Woods?'

'Near Austerlitz.'

'Near Austerlitz? Austerlitz?' It was like the empty echo of a child who is mentally handicapped.

'For Christ-sake why didn't you phone? You're staying in my house. I'm responsible for you.'

That was our word, Joachim's and mine. Not his. Responsible. I wanted to laugh. But I knew if I did he'd misinterpret the sneering twist to it, mistake it for mockery of him. Instead, I looked at him and sidetracked. The answer he'd expect from me. 'I'm a grown woman.'

'You have given me such trabble.'

'Trubble.' My response was automatic, though normally I relished such slip-ups.

'What?'

'I told you before, it's pronounced "trubble".'

'I am not in the mood. The next time you decide to disappear, you will have the courtesy to warn me in advance. It will save me a lot of time, effort and worry.' He spoke English as pedantically as he did everything.

'How'd you know I didn't go to the Institute?' I was finally curious.

'They phoned. I was on the point of reporting you missing when you knocked.' He continued to frown at me.

I threw him a filthy look. What he really meant was he'd been about to phone Joachim. Knowing what Joachim's reaction would be, my stomach began to churn as if it grappled with an excess of food, though I hadn't eaten since last night. I had got away in the woods today. For the first time. Hans would spoil it. Yet what could I expect? He had known Joachim long before me.

'Hans, I'm tired. Can I come in?'

He pulled me into the narrow hall and hustled me into the living room, like some wayward child. But after six years of Joachim's anger, I had developed a certain immunity.

'Whiskey? You're frozen.'

'Please.' Meekly. I'd give him no fuel. It would burn out quicker that way. It never worked with Joachim. But I'd seen it work with Hans.

I was taking the wild chestnuts out of my pockets when he came back.

'Where did you get those?'

'In the woods. Around Austerlitz.' Shit. I was under the microscope again.

'Tell me why you went there.' A psychiatrist humouring his patient.

I remembered the curve of the road, the shifting light in the trees, the quiet, dense duskiness of the path twisting through the woods. And the newness. I was safe in the newness. There was nothing to disturb me there.

'Well? Tell me, then.'

I searched for something to say, something he couldn't read into. I thought of the last few mornings, having breakfast with him and his cat, while his wife Leonie slept on obliviously upstairs: Hans buttering my bread, pouring my tea, forcing me to taste the curry-hot ginger marmalade; insisting on giving me Dutch lessons over breakfast, holding my coat, sending me off with a brusque wave and a brief smile. I had wallowed in the neat, shallow normality of it. An unexpected bonus in this respite from Joachim. I was grateful. But I couldn't afford to be honest. I knew he wanted me to tell him about the phone call. I looked at him, trying to gauge how much he'd overheard. His dark face told me nothing.

'Well?'

'Oh, I dunno. Maybe echoes of Napoleon.'

'Napoleon?'

I squirmed as he roared with laughter.

'Trust you. The right general, the right town, but the wrong country. The battle of Austerlitz was fought in Moravia, or what is now known as Czechoslovakia.' His eyes glinted. 'So what else did you find besides the ghost of a non-existent Napoleon?'

I avoided his face. 'Well.' I sipped my drink slowly and leaned to stroke the cat as she arched against my boots. I floundered on, trying to keep him distracted.

'Actually. I didn't quite reach Austerlitz. When it started to rain, I turned back.'

'Ha! Not what I asked. Though it partly answers my question. It seems you didn't quite reach anything today. Yet it's obvious that you and Joachim can't continue in this way.'

So. He'd heard enough of it.

'That's not fair. It's not that easy.' As soon as the words were out, I could have kicked myself. It would give him leverage.

'Facing reality never is. But it's easy to set out in the wrong direction for the wrong reasons and never arrive at your destination.'

I hated him.

'Then you see why I didn't phone. You'd no right to expect me to, since you seem to understand the circumstances so well.'

'Don't push it.' He stood, throwing back his head to drain the glass.

'Come. Set the table. The soup will be ready.'

I followed him to the kitchen and lounged against the door jamb while he cut the bread. He handed me the spoons. Inside, there wasn't room to swing his cat. His large frame was about as much as the tiny cubicle could accommodate.

'But did you find what you were looking for?' His voice followed me to the table.

I had been here six days. It was because of his friendship with Joachim that Hans had offered to put me up for the week while I attended the refresher course in Den Haag. Tomorrow evening I'd return to Joachim. I had to last till then. If only he hadn't called.

'The woods are very nice.'

'That's all?'

I jumped. He was close behind me, bare feet on the polished boards.

'Joachim phones you to torment you so much so that you don't sleep all night. Yes, I heard you. Today you disappear for ten hours, and now you tell me that the woods are nice. Please. Don't insult me.'

The steam from the bowls rose billowing so that his face was suspended, a disconnected entity before me. As she had been. My stomach rolled. Since that time I can no longer tolerate my food hot. Even my tea I take cold now, with ice and a punishing twist of lemon. The steam reminds me too much of the mist. Lately, smoke has also begun to affect me in this way.

We sat, his head and body welding as the steam dissipated. I tore a slab of bread, its crust snapping in the silence. He handed me one of the bowls of pea soup. Sea-green, it sucked on my spoon. I edged it aside and tried to ignore his scowl.

'Eat it.'

'I'm not hungry.'

'Eat it. It's nourishment.'

I dragged the bowl towards me, its sluggish contents vibrating faintly. There was nothing to be gained by resisting. He always won these confrontations over food. Besides. It was worth the pretence if it kept him from fishing.

'Well?'

I was wary again, sick of his questioning 'wells'. But he was nodding at the soup.

'All right if you like drinking peas. And don't tell me how it's one of your most famous national dishes.' The kind of banter he enjoyed.

'Your Irish stew can't hold a taper to it.'

I tried to clamp down on the sudden laugh which took me by surprise.

'It's funny, yes?' He was suspicious, then watchful when I

couldn't stop.

'You're close to hysteria.'

'Maybe you ought to slap my face,' I managed, wiping my eyes.

'I wouldn't presume. Joachim continues to do that efficiently enough for you.'

I stopped.

'How easily my kind of slap works.'

'Sadistic.'

He shrugged. 'Perhaps. But an effective remedy nevertheless. Though I'd prefer to examine the cause rather than keep staring at the effect.'

'You sound like a textbook.'

He grinned. 'Ja. A good textbook deals only in truth.'

'I didn't say you were good.'

'I'm more honest than you. You refuse to face anything.'

Jesus. I wanted to throw the soup in his face. I was sick looking inwards, sick facing it. I glowered at the remainder of liquid in the bowl. 'You don't know what you're talking about.'

'Joachim feeds on you.'

He was wrong. We feed on each other. All we have to sustain us is our guilt. That is our punishment and we depend on it.

'What happened while I was in the States? Joachim won't talk to me, and you, you flutter about like a half-starved sparrow. Come. Spit it out, for Christ's sake.'

'There's nothing. We've ... changed, that's all. You've been away a long time.' And he had. Six years had been long enough for us to bury it deep. And the move to Friesland had cut us off from those who knew. 'Anyway, what did you expect?' I gave him the level-eyed look I'd given the doctor the night he brought the pleasant, pipe-smoking psychiatrist. By now, I was well practised in uttering inanities to match the look. 'It's what being married does for you.'

'Crud!' The word hammered as he rose, fists slamming like mallets on the table. 'Nor am I fooled by that plastic smile. You ran away to the woods because of whatever Joachim said to you. But instead of facing the issue, you spin a cocoon of stupid slick phrases in which to conceal yourself.'

He leaned over to glare at me. 'Fool. Searching for answers

among the trees. Small wonder that you never arrived at Austerlitz.'

A fine spray of spittle pricked my bottom lip as I stared up at him. I'd never seen him so angry. He swept the dishes from the table, unmindful of the leftover soup slopping on the burnished wood.

Ignoring the mess, I stumbled back to the fire and hurled myself at the couch. Grinding my teeth, I watched the logs spit and hiss in the flames.

———

Leonie sat at the bar, drinking steadily. Mostly she ignored the man at her side as she concentrated on getting drunk. Occasionally, when he became too familiar, his thick fingers groping her thigh, she would turn to stare at him, pushing his hand impatiently from her. But she didn't tell him to go away. She hadn't made up her mind yet how she would play the evening. She wanted to confront them, but if she left it too late, the bitch would have gone to bed. Hans would wait up for her as always but if the bitch wasn't up, there would be no point in creating a scene. She'd learned that much with Hans. She could get at him through other people. The only way she could punish him now. It still stunned her that he felt no guilt. That was why she'd begun drinking. To torment him. That and her own guilt. But he was to blame. For all of it. He'd left her to decide. Washed his hands of it. But she knew if she'd had the kid, he'd have dumped her. Well, he'd pay for it. She'd make him. Until he felt it too. Already she was hacking at it, just as the thing had been hacked from her.

The man pushed another drink into her hand as she drained her glass and her lips drew back in a thin smile. The fourth one he'd bought her. His investment in the night. If she didn't agree to pay dividends he would turn ugly once they got outside the bar. It'd happened a couple of times before and she'd been frightened by it. Once she had even been hit. She didn't have much choice really. Glancing up at the clock over the bar, she saw it separate into two distinct globes that divided and fused in a crazy orbit every time she blinked. She made it out. Ten o'clock. Plenty of time. For both. She turned to the man who was muttering in her ear and nodded. He grabbed her bag and lifted her down from the stool.

I sat for a long time. Only when the couch creaked did I realise he was beside me. His fingers caught in my hair as he lifted it to see my face.

I stared at my knuckles, ignoring him. A log spat viciously, sparks threatening the worn rug that browsed on the hearth. The cat, unable to withstand the heat, lay wrapped in a corner of the couch.

'So. I've gotten to you.'

'Got.' I jumped at the chance. 'Gotten is an American corruption.'

'But it's acceptable, yes?' He was hooked. Or had he decided to let me off his?

'I checked it in the dictionary the last time. Even your Oxford allows for such Americanisms.'

Home ground. Lovely, safe, home ground. 'No such word as Americanism, either.'

'You are louse-picking.'

'Nit. Nit-picking. Never fails. You always crack under the strain of being corrected.'

'Louse.' He grinned and I tried to hide my relief.

'What d'you expect from a teacher of English?'

'An English teacher, then?'

'Oh, piss off Hans.' But I said it happily and he laughed as I'd anticipated. For all his finicky preoccupation with correctness, he delighted in the foreign flavour of such vulgarisms.

'I'm an Irish teacher of English.'

'But if I say you're an Irish teacher, it implies you teach Irish. How stupid is this language of yours.'

'You know it's not what I meant.'

'That is the trabble with you.'

'Trubble.'

'Whatever.' He raised a hand impatiently. 'You never say what you mean.'

I should have known. He had merely given me enough slack to recover. Now he was reeling in again. I tried to read what he was thinking as he leaned forward to pick a log from the stack in the wicker basket. I hadn't hoodwinked him, that much was obvious. But there was something else, only I was missing it.

He tossed the log, a smear of sap glinting in the lamplight before it hit the fire. We both drew back to avoid the flare of sparks that wheeled outwards. Normally, I liked the fires he lit. They never smoked. But this blaze was uncomfortable, stifling the air in the room.

'We used to dance wonderfully together, you realise, Leonie and I?'

Now where were we?

'Yet if I say "my dancing partner", you'll tell me it doesn't mean she's dancing right now, when we both know there is a strong possibility she's doing just that. You and your bloody grammar. Words.' He turned from the heat, suddenly furious. 'Stupid bumbling words, you make them mock what I want to say!'

So she was out. Returning this late, I'd assumed she was already in bed, sleeping soundly. I stuffed my hands between the rough knees of my jeans to hide their movement as I tried to think of an excuse to cut him short. I wanted to be up those stairs before she arrived.

'Why do you do that?'

'What?'

'Hide your hands. They're not noticeable, those small scars. Neither of you ever talks about it.' He was coming right at it.

Forgetting Leonie, I leaned towards the fire, out of the range of his eyes.

I managed a shrug. 'Nothing to talk about. A minor accident.' I paused, searching for bait to counter his. 'Anyway. What you were saying. It's semantics. Not just words, but what's implied in addition to their meaning. That's what you're arguing about.'

The couch groaned as he leaned back. 'More tricks? More words to hide behind? I'm baffled as to why you use language at all, since you avoid saying anything most of the time.'

I jumped up. 'You don't have a clue, you know that? Not a goddamn, fucking clue!'

'Yes?' He waited, impassive, and I almost bit. Almost. When he realised it was no good, his eyes flicked to my hands and I resisted the urge to put them behind my back.

'There.'

'My ass.' I held them out deliberately, palms upwards. 'Only a palmist would be disappointed in these.'

'I wasn't referring to the scars. It's the lack of gestures. You always used your hands, but now you keep them shoved in your pockets, or between your knees. Unnatural.'

Analytical Hans. I began to calm down. Standing would make it easier to escape the room. 'Just a habit, that's all.'

But he knew I was lying.

'Joachim phoned.'

So. It was the call which had upset him.

'When?'

'This morning.'

Watching for his reaction, I realised I was sitting again.

'What'd he want?'

His lips twisted. 'Whom, not what.'

I stared at the cat stretching ecstatically. 'What'd you tell him?'

'Unfortunately, he'd phoned the Institute and discovered you hadn't shown up today.'

'He phoned you to find out where I was.'

'Ja. But since he didn't at first reveal he knew you were missing, I said nothing.'

'You didn't tell him?' Hans covering for me. I gaped at him.

'Unfortunately.'

'What'd he say?' I tried to estimate the cost.

He grimaced, stretching long legs, lifting his bare feet to the heat. 'He was very angry. In fact, he exploded when I pointed out that he was the cause of your disappearance.'

His mouth stretched in a sudden sneer. 'It seems I'm no longer to be trusted where you're concerned.'

'That leaves me with nobody.'

'You can always leave him.' His voice was cold. 'The choice is yours.'

I stared at the scuff marks on my boots. 'I can't.' It was easier to control my voice when I kept it low. He was waiting for me to say something more but I stayed quiet.

The hall door slammed and even knowing what it meant, I was glad of its distraction.

'Leonie?'

Grim eyes on the living room door, he nodded.

An uneven clatter of stiletto heels sounded on the stone tiles in the hall.

'Is she ...?'

'Need you ask?' Still he watched the door.

There was no escape for me to the room above, except through the hall. Damn it. He hated me to witness the nightly drunken ritual. Even more than I did. I watched his face, immobile, as she tripped into the room. His gaze flickered once to take in her appearance, then shuttered. Reluctantly I turned.

She wasn't as drunk as usual. Her hair had escaped the tight severity of the chignon and lay in a black tangle about her. Something dark had splashed the front of her silk blouse and her left hand rubbed habitually at the stain. She carried a thorny-stemmed rose and for a moment the illusion that it wept in her hand was intense. But it was dried blood from several cuts and grazes.

She pointed at us, her voice shrill. 'I know what you're doing! I know what you ... are ... doing!'

She bent almost double as she pointed at the floor. 'Here. Right here. In my own house. Right under my nose.' She pushed her thumb hard against her left nostril, distorting her face. Christ. I closed my eyes then opened them to stare at the pinpricks of sweat outlining the scars on my hands.

Up to now she'd accused me of petty thievery. First it was her lighter. Then her tights. Now it was her husband. I turned to look at him as she continued raving. His stare was fixed on something beyond her. Then I realised he'd switched off to what she was saying. Waiting it out.

I sat, waiting with him, afraid to leave. If I attempted to go, she'd single me out as she'd done that first night.

The accusations, vulgar, vitriolic, spewed. But her anger was directed mainly at Hans. For a moment as I watched, an image of Joachim, eyes glittering, superimposed itself on Leonie. Though Joachim would never allow alcohol to spoil his performance.

I turned quickly to stare into the fire as she tottered towards us, eyes rolling. She never reached the couch. Hans jumped up, catching her as she fell. He lay her on the floor and eased her fingers open to remove the rose. There was blood in the palm of her hand.

Two could play. 'Hans, why do you —?'

'Quiet!' The word ripped into my question.

In the silence, I thought that was the end of it.

'She needs me.'

'And you?' I could have bitten my tongue off. He'd expect information in return.

He examined the inflamed skin. Slowly. Meticulously. When he found a thorn, he bent his mouth to her hand and sucked it free. He leaned low over her and spat into the fire, shadows leaping on his working jaw. When I'd begun to relax, thinking he wouldn't answer, he finally spoke.

'I need that.'

And his eyes. Stripped. Trapped in his own honesty. Then I knew. Whatever Leonie had become, it was because of him. Ashamed, I looked into the fire. But the log, a twisted charcoal, was no distraction. I was drawn again to watch him. Hans the mathematician, the logician. Like sap from the log. Like the rest of us.

He picked her up and swung her over his shoulder. The only way he could get her up the narrow stairs. He didn't return. I listened to the noises from above, the grey feather of ashes mounting in the grate. For a while I lay on the couch, the cat close to my head.

It'd been a mistake to come. In the long time he'd been away, I'd forgotten his tenacity. Tenacity. Still. Tomorrow I'd leave and he'd never know. Never know. Never know about the child. About the child that we killed. That we ... murdered. As though Joachim and I had placed our hands about her thin creased neck and throttled her. Just as effectively, as culpably as that.

I wouldn't tell Joachim how close Hans brought me to blurting it in that moment of anger. It would make him afraid if he thought my punishment might lessen. Only while the guilt weighed equally, could we continue. We'd agreed it after the inquest when no punishment was meted. That truck-driver. Poor snivelling bastard.

Tripping over himself to admit to it: yes he had been very tired; yes he might have dozed off at the wheel; yes he realised he'd veered onto the wrong side of the road; yes it was his fault and he was sorry sorry very very sorry. He took the blame. Willingly. We were responsible. But we let him take the blame.

Joachim's words when we carried her silence up from the dripping rocks: the driver sitting in the wet grass on the side of the dyke, heaving, his eyes dying in his face as he stared at her; the mist shrouding us, hemming us in.

'The fault is ours. Ours. We were arguing. You are not to blame.' The words swirled, amplified in the mist. But the driver was beyond hearing them. Later, when people came and raised his limp bulk, I saw the dark stain down his pants and wondered if he'd wet himself, or if it were just the moisture from the soaking marram grass. I preferred to wonder about that than to look at Joachim's face or to think of mine. Even when she'd materialised like a small icon, the filigree down of her hair dark with mist, he'd been silent, speaking only when I stopped screaming.

'We are responsible. There was time. We wasted it.'

Five days old. Within four hours of leaving the hospital, she was in its mortuary, awaiting the prodding fingers of the round, pink-veined pathologist. A birth and a killing. The filling between two Sundays. Filling our time in that filling. But worsening. Joachim staying longer each time in the blackness. Lasting weeks now. Weeks locked in his room, days when he won't eat, when the medication the doctor gives resignedly, remains impotent in his food. Then the white times. When he is fused with anger, when he seeks release in my skin and we come together, beating, beating. But there is no relief. And afterwards it is worse. Always worse. Just more tolerable than the blacknesses because time leaks a little faster. Like now. His anger on the phone. But one of us must work. We have to live. That is part of the punishment. The time must drip, Joachim said. He doesn't know for me it drips more slowly: he must never know the child belonged to Hans.

When I opened my eyes it was still dark outside. But it was morning. My last. There was no sound from upstairs and I breakfasted alone.

He was waiting when I returned in the evening, borne into the house on an icy blast that rattled the windows. He prowled the room as I rummaged in the hold-all.

'Do you want something to eat?'

I shook my head. 'I'll eat later with Joachim. Where's Leonie?'

'Asleep. She was drinking again this afternoon.' He stopped, glancing at the package in my hand.

'It's one of those porcelain jars for her collection.' I placed it gently on the table.

His lips tightened. 'Have you packed?'

'Practically. It'll only take me a couple of minutes to finish.'

'Hurry up. It's a long drive. He's expecting you by nine-thirty.'

I was afraid to ask if Joachim had phoned again. But his brusqueness annoyed me. I pounded upstairs, forgetting Leonie.

It was cold and dark outside. Breathing, it seemed we inhaled thin shards of ice. We waited for a gap in the continuous stream of cars. Suddenly he jerked me so that I lost my balance, my shoulder striking his chest. His breath hissed out furiously. I opened my mouth to apologise and closed it again. It was his doing. Then, before I could straighten properly, he was propelling me between the steaming cars.

We climbed into the Citroen, shivering in the cold, dark space. Our breaths quivered, condensing on the glass. I closed my eyes against it. When he didn't start the car I turned to look. He was staring into the fog on the windscreen.

'I can't get to Austerlitz,' I said, and waited.

'Nor I.' But he hated saying it.

I couldn't stand the fog and leaned forward to wipe the glass.

'Look at me.' His fingers bit my shoulder.

'The gift was not to placate Leonie, but to ease your conscience. You're aware of that, yes?'

I turned from the anger in his face.

'Answer me.' His voice ground, echoing Joachim's in its accusal.

'Yes.' And I recognised in the giving of the present that a new guilt had crept in. Insidiously. To add its weight even now, before we had resumed.

Damn you, Hans.

The Eavesdropper

Tiny Bill leaned forward, layers of fat resting on the counter. The bar stool appeared to be stuck up his ass.

'Quiet tonight, Jack.'

It was after midnight. The small stringy man behind the bar made a half-hearted nod, dropping his head forward to rest on his chest. 'Seems like it's just you and me again, Bub.' His voice was bitter. 'Jeez, this air. Brick-heavy.'

Tiny grinned. 'What's known as a Californian heat-wave.'

The heat steamed in the room, permeating everything, the ice fast extinguished in the rum he held before him.

Jack knew the question would come, but he waited, too enervated to move away. Tiny spoke the same words every night, drinking the responses with the air of a parched man.

'Sally not in yet?'

'Nope.' He emptied the slops from the drip tray into the sink, wrinkling his nose against the pungent stench of beer.

'Been late a lot lately.'

'Huh.' Jack didn't want to think about it. Fuck her.

'Kinda miss her about the place. Got a great sense a humour, that gal.' Tiny laughed. 'No kidding, but she's one helluva dame.'

'Huh.' Jack polished a glass till it squealed, his owlish eyes catching the wink of burnished wood under the lights.

'You two getting on okay?'

Jack grunted.

'How're them classes a hers going?'

He poured himself a drink. 'How in hell would I know! She ain't here often enough to have a proper conversation with no more.'

'Hey up! I didn't mean nothing.' Tiny pushed his glass forward, nodding for a refill. "Sides, I'm your pal, right? You and me, we go way back. Why, I remember —'

'It ain't you, Tiny.' Jack sloshed the rum into the fat man's glass. 'This fucking heat. Goddamn it, where in hell is she!'

'What's it tonight, aerobics?'

'If it ain't that, it's something else. Look at the frigging clock!'

'Y'know, maybe you shouldda done what she wanted that time.'

'Huh?'

'Jazzed up the place a little, brought in some a those country 'n western boys to attract the customers. Then she couldda helped out in the bar, like she'd wanted.'

'Draw trouble, y'mean. I ain't going looking for trouble.' The bar was in a rough part of town, the quiet decor and piped orchestra his weapons against a boisterous clientele. So far he'd been lucky.

'It mighta kept her home nights. You two been together a good while. I'd hate to see —' Tiny stopped, catching the look on Jack's face. 'Aw, women! Fuck 'em. They're only good for one thing.' He laughed, the layers of fat vibrating. 'And I just said what it is.'

'If I could get it. She's always asleep by the time I go up, that stinking grease smeared all over her face.'

'Shit, Jack. You too easy on her. I never let no woman call the shots with me. Make it a double.' He nudged his glass again.

'Hitting it hard tonight.' Jack poured.

'What the hell. I got nothing to save myself for. I'll tell you something, Jack. Best little lady in the world's a bottle of rum. Never lets you down.' Tiny had once been married. It had lasted five years. From then on he'd never bothered with women. Or they hadn't bothered with him. Peering back at the years through a haze of alcohol, he was no longer sure which.

'You oughta drink a bit more. Relax. Nothing like booze to kill those cravings. Honest truth pal, I can't even remember the last time I wanted a woman.' Tiny's words were beginning to slur. He'd be hard to shift when it came closing time.

Hearing the door thrust inwards, Jack looked up expectantly. It wasn't Sally. He made to look away, but something about the couple jolted him. The woman had a dazed expression. Jack wondered if she were spaced out on something but he stiffened as he caught the look of the man. Trouble. He copped it in the quick eyes straining for the same kind of release that the jutting shoulders sought through the shirt seams. He cursed silently. The man was too big for him to handle. He pictured the phone on the shelf behind him and hoped when it came, there would be time.

The man strode to the bar as the woman wandered between the tables.

'What can I get you, Bub?' Jack hadn't meant to say 'Bub'. In his nervousness, it had slipped out.

The man glanced at him coldly, eyes the colour of wet slate. 'Two Scotch.'

'On the rocks?'

He jerked his head abruptly, anger stored in his teeth. He stared past Jack at the woman in the huge mirror behind the bar, watching her blunder into tables as she approached.

'What'd you do?' Her words were flat, each weighing equally with the next. She climbed onto the stool. Her hair was pinned up but several streals had escaped. There was no comprehension in her eyes, only a bewilderment that suggested she couldn't relate what she saw to what it might mean.

'How many times?' His voice was glass grinding, and Jack edged away. Tiny was staring into his drink. Jack poured a generous measure of Scotch and gulped it back. A pair of oddballs, he decided, feeling calmer as the whiskey lined his fear.

The heat quivered in the wings of the electric fans. What the place needed was air-conditioning but he couldn't afford it yet. He lifted a cloth and wiped his face. Realising it was the glass rag, he glanced surreptitiously at the couple to see if they'd noticed. The man had pulled the woman's hair back from her forehead and was pressing his thumb hard on a dark bruise where the temple met the hairline. The woman didn't even whimper. She stared at the man as though she were blind. Jack shivered, not knowing what to do. Down the other end of the bar, Tiny was engrossed in lighting a cigarette. He'd already set fire to it half-way along and smoke was steaming from its side as he tried to find the end. Several matches lay burnt out on the counter.

Jack moved quickly, scooping the matches, examining the smooth wood.

'You lost something, pal?' The glazed eyes brightened for an instant amid the mounds of flesh.

'Nope.'

'Sally not here yet?'

Jack grimaced and moved away. The man was lifting the woman from the stool. They were leaving. Terrific. He uncurled his fists. But his relief was short-lived. The man pulled the woman to him and began a slow gyration to the music. The woman made no effort to dance, letting him drag her about. She was nicely rounded but it was hard to tell her limpness from a rag doll. Jack wanted to tell them dancing wasn't allowed, he didn't have a licence. But he didn't have the guts.

The man bent his head and said something to the woman. She didn't answer. Jack watched the stain spread across his sharp features, the swift flex of muscles co-ordinating into one mass that drew back slightly as though preparing to strike. Like a panther. Or a snake. The threat as palpable as the heat. Jack blinked, trying to swallow but the parched walls of his throat folded. He reached instinctively for the phone.

Suddenly the woman slumped, placing her head on the man's shoulder. Relieved, Jack turned to the mirror. He caught a glimpse of the man's hands sliding down the woman's back to stroke her ass. He turned, wanting to call out, 'Hey, none of that tomfoolery in here,' but his mouth went slack. Transfixed, he watched the woman's buttocks being lifted and kneaded. He wriggled a little, trying to lessen his sudden discomfort as he recalled the feel of Sally's skin.

The man released the woman so abruptly she staggered backwards against a table. He jerked his head in Jack's direction, his eyes flaking the expression on the bartender's face, the dull flush of his skin. He knew. Jack tried to turn away, but the man's eyes pinned him with a callous amusement. Without looking at the woman, he spoke to her, 'You play your cards right, you got another one here all raring to go.' His smile was ugly.

'Same again. Bub.'

Bristling at the sneer, Jack turned to prepare the drinks. The frigging prick. Someone oughta smash his face in. Visions of a bloodied mouth spitting teeth calmed him. He'd have to sweat it out. Yeah, sweat. The clean shirt he'd put on earlier was sticking to his back and already he could feel the clammy warmth in his armpits. Where the fuck was Sally?

He glanced quickly at the woman. Lipstick splashed her mouth, tiny stains of it seeping in the corners above her upper lip. Her whole appearance suggested she hadn't used a mirror. Maybe that was why she was staring so hard at her own reflection. Jack felt the man's eyes on him and turned quickly to ring the change.

'What'd you do?' The same words, leaking sluggishly from the woman's mouth, their tone buoying Jack's spirits. For some reason his spirits always lifted when he heard the dull beat of misery in a voice. On nights like that, he could mount the stairs whistling, happy in the belief that his lot was not so bad.

'Kinda hard to believe but time was when that fink was bigger 'n me,' the man was saying. 'When we were kids. 'Cept even then, he couldn't swing a punch. Too chicken-livered.' The snarling edge to the man's laugh gnawed at Jack's bladder. He took some glasses over to the shelves below the mirror and sneaked a look.

'He ever tell you what happened his hamster? Frigging little pest was always chawing my stuff. I warned him to keep it locked up, outta my stuff or he'd be sorry. Well, he was sorry okay.' The man paused, shaking a cigarette from a pack. Jack saw something flicker in the woman's eyes, then her face closed. But the dazed look was gone and the man's lips twisted.

'You ever pressed flowers? Nice 'n flat so's you can make pictures with them? Our maw used to make flower pictures. Boy, was I sick of those pictures. Every goddamn wall in the house — like she discovered a new kinda wallpaper. You ever seen a flower press? Our maw had one. Big solid pieces a wood with four thick bolts. For screwing and tightening.'

Something in the way the woman's eyes came alive, flying to the man's face, made Jack uneasy. The man turned to her, the thin blade of his nose stabbing the air at her face.

'Yeah, tightening, 'n squashing, 'n flattening.'

The woman waved her arm vaguely, as though to fend him off. The man caught her wrist and held it, his hand matted with hair. Jack felt the clammy lick of sweat on his skin, seeing finally what the woman saw. He tried to move away as the voice ground on, raucous in the heat. But he couldn't. His legs felt weak and he placed his hands on the shelf, gritting his teeth as the memory swamped him, the dark leaping at him, mottling his own image in the glass: he was back again suffocating in it, the impenetrable blackness clawing his face, Doyle's voice outside screaming, 'Snake's in there. He's gonna get you. He's gonna squeeze you good and proper, you slimy rat-fink!' He heaved, fighting to regain control. It was seldom now it started up, tearing his gut. Over and done with, he'd have to remember. But as he stared in the glass he knew he was fooling himself. The mirror trapped it, told it like it was: a thin balding man who was afraid. Like it always was. Always would be. The fear keeping him apart, making him a faint reflection of what he should be. As though he weren't real. As though he had no substance other than an image trapped in two mirrors angled to repeat his reflection backwards and forwards, smaller and smaller. He blinked to shut it out. But he couldn't: what had been was stranded in his face, would be there again tomorrow. Fuck this prick and his sick talk reminding him. His gaze shifted to the couple.

The man's mouth had tightened in a harsh slit, teeth forcing the words, low and guttural. 'How many times?'

Jack jumped as the woman exploded to life. Sliding down, she raced for the door. The man swung from the stool, striding after her. Jack stood gaping as the door crashed behind them.

Even the heat seemed less for their absence. Trembling, he splashed some whiskey into a glass and drained it. At the other end of the bar, Tiny's expression was rapt, blinking cross-eyed at the air before him. He screwed his face up and his eyes were swallowed in a fleshy swamp. Time Jack got him sober enough to make it out the door.

He was brewing the coffee when the door opened. He swung around, jittery, the couple still on his mind. But it was Sally. Finally. At two in the morning. His eyes narrowed as he watched her unsteady swing towards the bar. Tight as hell. This was a new development and he didn't know what he should do.

'Hi, you guys. Sorry I'm late.' Her voice was surprisingly tin-selly, as if the alcohol had by-passed her tongue. She made several attempts to get up on the stool, but her foot kept missing the rung. She reached out and sank her hand in Tiny's shoulder, levering herself up. Tiny turned, twitching his great heap as though he were dusting a fly.

'Sally?' He strained blearily. 'You been here long?'

She laughed, the sound grating on Jack's ears.

'Yeah, all night. How you doing, Tiny?'

Jack set the cups carefully on the beer mats. For the first time he looked directly at her.

'Where you been?'

'I tell you the one about the drunk seeing double?' Tiny began, then frowned as he tried to remember the joke. He picked up his cup absent-mindedly.

'Murphy's. A gang of us went to hear the singing.'

'Who else?' He knew she wouldn't answer him straight. She never did when she saw he was mad at her.

'Who else what?' She was perched on the stool like a small bird, the pull of skin on her forehead as she raised her brows making her slightly bulbous eyes protrude further. Like a bullfrog. Jack lowered his eyes in disgust.

'Who else went?' He poured more coffee for Tiny. Sally hadn't touched hers.

'Oh, everyone. You know.' Fumbling to light a cigarette, she wouldn't look at him.

Jack felt something collapse inside him but he couldn't leave it. Something about the man and woman in the bar earlier, something he wasn't quite sure of, made him want to keep on. Besides, it was happening too often. He poured himself a half-glass of whiskey.

'If I knew, I wouldn't a asked.'

She looked at him all innocence, her permed curls bobbing as she cocked her head. She pecked at the cup, then made a face, pouting her lips. Her latest craze was to look like Shirley Temple, though she was middle-aged. The effect was ... obscene. The word came suddenly out of nowhere, shocking him. He looked at her, confused, remembering the quiet, timid Irishwoman who had moved in with him, as grateful as he to escape the loneliness. Now with her new looks, her phony American accent, he hardly knew her.

'But sweetie, you know them. The whole crazy gang.' She laughed. 'That time you told me to bring them back after class. What a night! They still talk about it.'

Yeah, he remembered. Run off his feet pumping booze into her friends. Friends! He felt a stab of resentment. Since when had she graduated from Miss Mouse to Miss Popularity? And that blond All-American plastic shit breathing down her neck, whispering in her ear, dirty talk, he was sure of it from the way she had simpered and giggled.

'All the men go too?'

'Sure. Why not? Hey, Tiny, how you doing?' Her elbow disappeared in the crook of Tiny's arm as she poked him.

'I tell you the one about the drunk —'

Thinking of the way the man had treated the woman earlier, Jack spoke. 'I don't want you going noplace with them no more.' He put the glass down to still the rattle of ice.

She turned to look at him, her face bland. 'Why not?'

Any hope he might have had plummeted.

'I want you home is why.' He cringed inwardly as she heard the pleading note in his voice. It was coming out all wrong. He had wanted to sound strong, even bossy.

'Home? Me upstairs in those rooms going crazy while you serve a handful a customers nights? Or me downstairs propping up the bar with Tiny here, filling time? Which kinda home d'you mean?'

'I know it's not —'

'Yeah you know, you know. But there ain't a goddamn thing you're gonna do about it so stop picking on me.' She turned from him. 'Yeah, about the drunk, Tine ...' She shook him gently to wake him up. Jack turned away, catching his despair in the mirror. He gripped his glass and threw the rest of its contents down his throat, almost choking on a cube of ice. Listening to Tiny, he ground the ice between his teeth.

'... seeing everything double. When he gets to the john, he sees he has two triggers. So he puts one back in his pants and pees all over himself.'

Sally laughed louder than normal, her voice an acute screech that probed the inside of his head. He spun around, grabbing her shoulders. 'You with that phony stud?' He glared at her, trying to find the lies in her face.

Sally stopped laughing, her mouth hanging wide. He could see all the way to the back of her throat, the flesh pink and moist, shutting him out as she worked to speak. 'What in hell're you on about? What phony stud?'

'Don't gimme that crap. That fink with the big teeth like a row a Steinways. You know damn sure.'

'Ron? You gotta be kidding.' She stared past him. He knew then, saw it in the way her eyes kept shifting, looking at anything except him. God, how he wished he'd never asked her. The pain seemed to reach the furthest parts of his body.

'You goddamn whore!' The words ground, echoing the tone of the man who had come into the bar earlier.

'You're not kidding.' She said it quietly but her face went cold and stiff. She pulled away from him, dropping awkwardly from the stool. 'If that's what you think, maybe we oughta split for a while.' She patted the fat man on the shoulder. ''Night Tine.'

Jack was trembling. 'Where you going? We gotta talk.'

'Don't wanna talk now. Tomorrow. I'm going to bed.' She swung unsteadily towards the door that led to the stairs and the rooms above.

Jack closed his eyes. At least she hadn't left. Yet. The word stabbed him.

'You been fighting with Sally? Where's my favorite gal?' Tiny roused himself, squinting at the empty seat beside him.

Jack felt it happening slowly. A heat that smoked like the tinder on the scorched hills, igniting as he recognised the latest addition to Tiny's repertoire; its promise to stare him down the nights.

'C'mon. Time you hit the road.' In his fury, he got rid of Tiny in half the time it normally took, slamming the door on the warm dark night. He poured himself another drink. He still couldn't believe it. He tried to wish he'd kept his mouth shut. But he couldn't, his anger against her was too big and noisy in his head.

Anyway, it was pointless. He'd known it for weeks, tried to stifle the growing suspicions. Tonight or some other night. What was the difference? Only he'd helped her say it. He caught a muffled sound from above, and the panic expanded. She couldn't leave. Not yet. Not before he ... What? He listened, calming as the silence settled above, the hatred creeping in.

He pictured her in bed the way she always slept, lying on her side, one arm thrown out over the cover, exposing her small white shoulder: her white childish shoulder. Bruiseless. He had never hurt her. The thought spiked his anger as he remembered the dark bruise on the woman's forehead and the man's thumb pressing it. The bitch. The frigging bitch, she couldn't, he wouldn't let ...

He turned swiftly to pick up the whiskey bottle, stiffening as the mirror caught him. He stared, his heart lurching. The image looming in the glass was not his. He was looking into the face of the man who had been in the bar earlier. The features were vaguely recognisable as his own, but the anger, the hatred, the cruel eyes were not his. Not his.

He sweated, fighting the mirror as though the man in the glass were more real than he. There were other ways to go. Other ways? What ways? his eavesdropper taunted. She's leaving, pal. Know what it'll be like after she's gone? Jack saw the years unravel in the glass, saw Tiny's way of coping; the monotonous days chalked by the inane words of his customers, soured with the bitterness spiked by the fat man's questions. And he felt the fear inside him, the fear that would reach from the past to grasp his throat every time the bar door swung to admit a man who sensed his jittery control.

He couldn't face that. Wouldn't. Not again. Ever. Watching the image, he saw the fear fuse to a hard core of hatred. He was surprised at his sudden calm, the sensuous feeling that he bathed in the aftermath of something. Like that time when he was little and he blew in the bullfrog's mouth with a straw. The power that had flowed through him. It was here now, as though the years of feeding slyly on reflections had somehow shattered his body, leaving an untouchable him cloned in the mirror. Safe from the fear. He reached out, laying his hand on its surface, feeling the flow of hatred from his glass fingertips through the axis into his flesh. The fear could stay in the glass. To prod him. But there was no room for it in his body. His body had substance.

Smiling, he turned, remembering the glass in his hand. Still some whiskey in it. He loosened his fingers, letting it fall to the floor he kept scrupulously clean. It did not smash, landing on the thickness of its base. The spilt whiskey snaked across the tiles. Snaked. He watched it. Then he lifted his foot and brought it down hard. The glass burst, squealing against the ceramic floor as he crunched it. He scraped his foot on the tiles with the tiny splinters embedded in his shoe until he stepped on the carpet outside the bar.

Appeasing the Beast

Eve sleeps. But lightly, so that when he comes, her dreaming dreams him noiseless as a panther skulking in the bowels of the house, the ritual of coffee percolating the walls as he prepares.

But it is the child's cry ringing out suddenly, then stilling, which wakes her fully to it.

She shivers, the ache in her head faltering in the sudden onslaught of a spasm wracking her body. More than any other sign, it is the pain which proves the most precise monitor of how far she's advanced towards the final stages.

He will take five minutes forty-five seconds to sip the coffee, twenty-one seconds to take the stairs two at a stride and cross the musty landing, three seconds to place his hand on the knob which will scratch as he turns it, opening the door: in all, three hundred and sixty-nine throbs of pain before he will enter the room.

Already the heaviness is ebbing from her limbs so that the damp weight of the cloth across her eyes commits her to a chill deep well of darkness where pain is relentless, an iridescent scream indistinguishable from its own lingering echo.

She lies, as she has always lain, the tears seeping inwards while she waits for him to come.

———

Mama is sick. Mama's sick, sick, so sick.

Are you listening Mr Fox. Drink your coffee and listen. No. Too many spoons you can't have, sugar is bad for your teeth. Bad, bad, so bad. It'll make you sick. No not Mama-sick, toilet-sick, all yellow and sticky and bad-smelling. And your teeth'll rot and fall out dead. And the fairies won't give you any pennies because you've been a bad girl Mr Fox. So bad. It is not too hot, drink it. If you don't drink it I shall pull your sore arm right off and then it'll have to stay off because Mama's too sick to sew it back on and Dadda Owen's too busy minding her.

All your stuffing'll fall out, all over the table and the floor and then what'll you do. You'll just go dead so dead and I'll have to put you in a no-breathing box, see. Now stop it. Stop crying.

Don't cry now, don't. Oh don't, I won't hurt you, really I won't. I was only pretending, look, cross my pigtails and smile. Oh stop it oh please oh don't cry, here, wipe your nose. Oh really really I'm sorry forgive forgive me Mr Fox I love you. Don't you know I wouldn't really pull off your arm and make you die and be all alone, didn't I cry more than you when Dadda Owen caught your arm in the door didn't I didn't I.

And didn't I kiss you better all over you, all over and over just like Dadda Owen kissed me to make my bad go away far far away into a black hole and never come out again.

———

Outside the door, footfalls soft as sighs. It is time, time appointed. Is, was, will be, forever now at the hour of remembered breath.

Eve shudders as he enters, the door closing behind him, its sound inexorable as the rattle of clay on wood.

He does not come to her immediately but crosses to prepare the final injection, his shoes staccato on the bare boards.

She sucks in the sounds, scavenging among them to grasp the debris of memory.

When he comes to the bed and kisses her, she tastes it on his tongue with the coffee, the acrid bite of the whiskey he's laced it with. The needle pricks her arm and almost instantly torpor courses again, invading her limbs swiftly as a conquering army. But though the Pentothal lessens her capacity to feel, still the pain holds her in thrall.

His breath burns the hollow of her throat as he leans across her, placing the syringe in the kidney dish. In the quiet, the faint scratch of needle against steel confirms his action.

Soon, she thinks, soon, and there is fear threading the thought.

———

You're not Dr Fox, where's Dr Fox.

Yes I know you're a real doctor, I'm not stupid, you know. No,

I don't want to talk about Dr Fox, who's Dr Fox, I don't know anyone by that name.

Did I, I didn't. Well ... maybe your nurse said Dr Fox, after all it's a big hospital, there must be a Dr Fox somewhere. Please, I don't want to, I don't want to look at the dolls. Because. Just because, that's all. I'm too big now to play with dolls, stupid things all bumps and sticks.

No thanks, I hate coffee, hate hate it. No reason, I just do. Please let me go, I'm not mad you know, it's awful here, you don't know what it's like, the woman in the next bed keeps emptying her dinner in my locker oh it's awful, oh please, please, I can't bear it, Auntie May would have me back, I'm sure she would if you asked her.

Yes but I haven't hurt myself here, see, not even once, did you tell Auntie May that, did you, I didn't mean to frighten her, I didn't mean to scald myself, really I didn't, the coffee pot just got in my hand ... somehow ...

I don't remember what I thought.

I said I don't remember. A ... a bad dream, I'm sure that's what it was.

You know that, why are you asking me when you have it all written down, Mama got sick and died that's all, three-six-nine-your-Mama-is-a-dyin'-'n-I'm-lonely-oh-so-lonely-sad-and-lonely-Clementine. Nothing, nothing, just some stupid rhyme.

I told you before I don't remember him, he wasn't my real father. I don't remember, I was too small, see. I don't know why he went away. Please, just let me go, will you, I promise I'll be good. Good good so good, if you'll just let me go.

The narcotic reigns in Eve's body, its languorous hold wielding utter dominion.

In her ears the rasp of fabric against skin as he removes his clothes.

When he straddles her, the mattress buckles beneath his weight. The pain eats into her scalp as he tightens the blindfold, the cold damp band of cloth pressing her gaze into that which is ever present.

His tongue roams her skin, bearing the breath of coffee and alcohol.

When he pushes into her, despite her torpor, she bucks against the force of the invasion. There is no palpable rhythm as he moves in her, only the cut and thrust of memory made flesh, laying siege to her body in a bed of bumps and sticks.

Descending to the deepest regions of the well she inhabits, time is presence beneath her skin, his sweat sealing her pores in the manic jig of release.

———

But I'm better, you even said to Auntie May I was much better, she told me on the phone yesterday oh please let me go back to her, she needs me to help her do the shopping and carry things she can't manage all on her own in that big old house oh please.

Improving, she didn't say improving, she said much better that's what she said you said.

But they're only little ones tiny scratches that's all, I told you, I fell in the bushes this morning, it was all an accident, the thorny bushes over near the vegetable plot, I was just going for a walk and I wasn't looking where I was going and and I fell that's all really I swear.

Yes I'm listening.

I am I am listening.

I did not do it on purpose. I did not.

I didn't, why would I do that, hurting hurts, see.

But I don't have any big pain inside I told you, oh I promise I promise I'll look where I'm going I won't hurt myself again, ever.

I don't remember Mama being sick, I don't I'm tired telling you, tired tired, you're the one that's fucking mad. Mad mad you're just so fucking mad.

How should I know I don't remember.   ,

Well if Auntie May says I called him that then maybe I did. Because, well, she told me he wasn't my real father, how else could I know when I don't remember.

I don't want to say it, that's the why.

No.

No.

Because, that's all.

Alright alright, Dadda Owen, there, are you happy now. Stupid, stupid saying it, as if I was a baby or something.

I don't remember him going away the night Mama died, if you want the truth I think Auntie May's lying about that.

I don't know why, I just do, see, that's all.

Well, maybe she got mixed up how would I know, I'm not saying she's lying on purpose or anything Auntie May would never do that, oh please let me out of this place, I've been here so long so very long, please let me go back to her.

What story there is no story I don't know what you're trying to make me say.

Yes you are you're trying to make me say I don't know, something, what is it, you're pushing pushing as if there's something there, only there isn't there isn't there's nothing there, what do you want me to do, make something up, is that what you want.

———

Eve waits in the dark while he dresses. He checks the number of bank notes before shoving them in his pocket where the key she has given him nestles.

Even now, after so long, he still cannot bring himself to trust her though she has never yet shortchanged him just as she has never cheated any of the men who came before him. Yet in other respects he has proved himself perfect, loyal as a besotted lover in fulfilling her every request.

Even when he leaves, padding to the door in his socks, she does not move.

She lies listening as he descends the stairs, some creature large and secretive, stealing from the old house.

Only when the hall-door resounds in his wake, its single, definitive toll sending shock-waves through the empty rooms, does she finally remove the blindfold.

The release is swift. Her eyes fill, tears spurting with total abandon from the stream of pubescent infant days.

For a little while it is over, her demon sleeps. There will be weeks of relief, blank pain-free weeks washed clean of desire before he reawakens, ravenous as he stalks her blood, commandeering the old story.

Only then will she need the man to come again.

When the pain in her head has eased to a pulse, she opens her eyes, squinting against the shock of light from the bulb. Rising, she folds the robe about her, secreting the stale sweat of old treacheries.

Tomorrow she will return to work. She will dress wounds, bathe skin, soothe fears, shave hair, inject drugs, take blood, cool brows, wipe sweat, hold dying hands, listen to the puttering rattles of breath, all for a wage that will buy him when her need rears again, when the beast must be appeased.

———

Hello. Fine thank you. See see, still no marks at all, it's been a long time now, I haven't hurt myself at all, see, now maybe you'll begin to believe me about the thorns.

Great, it was great, we made it up between us, I told Auntie May I was sorry I'd frightened her, I told her I'd never do anything to frighten her again. I showed her my arms and legs, look, I said, no marks, I should be at school, I'm missing all my lessons, I want to go back to school, I want to go home, please take me home. And she hugged me and we cried and cried. I was afraid the nurse would come and stop the visit, but she didn't, she left us alone and Auntie May promised she'd ask you to let me go home for a week-end, did she ask you did she, oh please say you'll let me, I'm sorry about being rude to you all those times, oh I feel so happy today, I didn't even mind when Amelia emptied the gravy in my bed, Nurse Costello got really mad, poor Amelia.

I wish I could tell you, I really wish I could, but I really can't remember about him and Mama, I can't.

Well, sometimes I think I remember her being sick in a big high bed, lying quiet and still for a long time, but I can't remember him going away and Auntie May coming and finding me trying to wake Mama up, I've thought and thought but I really can't remember, you've got to believe me, when Auntie May told me about that, well, I just spilled the coffee and and scalded, I got a fright, see, a big fright just hearing it like that, we were sitting at the kitchen table and she was showing me some pictures in the old album, Mama when she was young, standing outside this big hotel some-where, and then she, Auntie May, she just kind of blurted it, out of the blue, she never said anything before, see, not once, and another thing I think, well, about Mama being sick and the big high bed, Auntie May says that's how it was but I don't know, I don't know if I think I remember it just because she told me, I've thought and thought and I just don't know and that's the truth. And I don't remember him, really I don't, I was too small, see. Oh please say I can go home for the week-end, I want to get better I want to get better as fast as I can, Auntie May needs me the drains are stuffed with leaves again and she can't manage the ladder or carrying the coal scuttle she needs someone to look after her.

Crossing to the window, Eve hauls backs the old brocade to stare out. But the dark-absorbed glass relinquishes only her own image silhouetted against the room's interior. She presses forward, staring down through herself at the city, its galaxy of lights brazening the sky, beyond Howth, the sea vanishing into darkness. The cemeteries too are unlit. They, like the sea and the dead, are vanquished. She pictures the grave, the single anniversary rose she has placed beneath the headstone this morning.

A long time gone now Mama, and still you are. Are, were, will be, forever now at the hour of remembered breath.

Happy Breathday to you Happy Breathday to you Happy Breathday Dear Mama Happy wake wake up Mama why don't you wake up see see what Mr Fox and I have made you coffee Mama coffee here drink drink it Mama why won't you drink oh please Mama move your lips where's Dadda Owen I can't find him is he gone away Mama I'm glad glad he he hurt Mr Fox Mama he hurt her real bad bad bad so bad oh please Mama wake wake up I promise I'll be good I'll be a good girl I'll be good for Dadda Owen I promise I won't be bad I won't scream I won't I'll never never never scream again oh please wake up Mama please I'm sorry sorry sorry forgive me oh please I love you Mama.

Eve swivels from the memory, the walls wheeling as she stumbles to escape the room. On the landing, she clings to the banisters, hauling the must of decades into her lungs.

When the house steadies about her, she descends to the kitchen. On the table lies the rest of the intravenous phials she has stolen from the hospital, beside them the cassette machine on which he has played the child's cry. She tidies them away and makes tea, the triviality of such chores balm to that which she cannot heal, the wound she tends with diligence, swabbing and dressing it in what is the only compromise.

Body Found on Waste Ground

His three days leave was up. In less than an hour he would board the bus at the edge of the township, first passing through the military checkpoint, eyes averted as the South African police scanned his identification papers, his working permit.

He was back in it again — the little plastic egg-timer he'd once seen in the window of an Indian store. As if his flesh, his bones, had been ground to minuscule grains of sand, wantonly tossed backwards and forwards through the narrow waist of the glass. The wait had begun, the endless spilling of the hours before his next trip home.

'Almost time.' His wife's voice reinforced it.

Turning from the window, the cloud tendrils streaking like tearsmoke, the unnatural quiet of the street, he faced her. Like the women of the Xhosa, she was small, statuesque, the full fleshiness of her body coming more from a diet of mealie porridge and bread than from any inherited tribal characteristics.

'Is there time?' He wanted her again, the sudden need spiking from the empty months he saw stretching ahead of him in the single men's hostel outside Kimberley.

Olla shook her head. 'Enough. I'm too sore.' She smiled to soften it and he saw she wanted to cry. But she wouldn't. Not until he was gone. She kept her head down, her small hands flitting to wrap the bread he would eat on the ride through the night. The air was leaden, the sun driving the heat through the metal roof. He paced the hut, edgy now, his shoes snapping on the concrete as he walked to the curtain. Reaching under, he felt for the small holdall and was startled when he touched the heat still trapped where they had lain on the mattress. He leapt up as the door burst open, but it was his daughter, at seventeen, a slight version of her mother.

'You're early?' Olla was suspicious, pausing as she carried tea to the makeshift table.

Brown eyes went to her mother's face, avoided her father's. Nkulie could not bear the skeletal look of him. Worse each time he came from the mines.

'They were at it again.'

'Godfrey?' Her parents spoke together.

'Okay. At the church for choir. He was lucky. Their bloody Casspirs surrounding the place. They threw tear gas at the younger ones playing in the school yard. And laughed. They took Sipho away.' She hurled the plastic bag she carried her books in, landing it on the neatly rolled rush mats in the corner where she slept with her younger brother.

'You stay out of it. All you've got to worry about is those exams.' Thabo sipped the mug of milkless tea, looking at the daughter he hardly knew.

'Didn't you hear me? They took Sipho!' Nkulie stared at her mother, biting her lips.

Olla nodded. 'Listen to Baba. You can't help Sipho now.'

'I'm going to inquire.'

'Stay away.' Thabo slammed the tin cup on the loose boards. 'That time I went to the station to look for Modise? They almost detained me as well.'

'He'll be tortured. You don't care!'

Thabo lifted one of the boards from the concrete blocks, smashed it down. 'I can't afford to! If I lose this job —'

'The Comrades would help us.'

'A bunch of hungry students looking for trouble.'

'Food parcels for the old, the sick? Campaigning for detainees? Finding homes for those evicted?'

'If they would stick to that. But no, they have to protest. Look where it's got them. Dying like flies. For what?' Thabo wiped the sweat from his eyes, his whole body sticky and uncomfortable.

'For liberation. To free us from the chains of white slavery, white imperialism, white oppression. War together, children! Liberation before education, an idea whose time has arrived.' Nkulie sang, the tight curls of her hair dancing.

Thabo sucked in his cheeks, fighting for control. He felt the skin tighten across his back. He could barely write his own name. Even that small dignity was thanks to Olla, the schooling she'd had growing up on one of the white farms outside King Williams Town. He was proud too of his daughter's education. But she'd been at it ever since he'd arrived, slinging words he hardly knew the meaning of. He was sick with fear at what it meant.

'Funeral words! For every one of those there's a bullet or the lash of a sjambok. You think I go down that stinking mine shaft, sleep in that stinking compound with thirty other men day and night day and night for nine months so you learn to talk like this? The exams can give you a future —'

Nkulie's lips whitened. 'Those bloody Boers will make sure there are no exams. They're looking for a reason to close the schools.'

'You're giving it. They'll hound you.'

'We've always been hounded. Look at the way we live. Is this a life? A tin hut? A cold water tap for every hundred families? A toilet shared by two hundred? What are we? Blacks? Dirt? What?'

'Enough!' Olla moved to her daughter, shaking her fist. 'Don't tell us how we live. If it gives you an education, then it's worth it. You've upset Baba. Tell him now, before he goes. You'll stay away from the Comrades. Tell him, daughter.'

Nkulie's lips clamped, a closed beak as she went to sit on the rush mats in the corner. She tore a book from the bag and began turning pages.

Olla sighed. For Thabo's sake she would pretend.

'There, you see. She listens to us. Ah, what is talk? Nothing to be afraid of. Children's talk. Now, your papers?'

Nkulie watched her mother fussing. As soon as he was gone, Olla would go behind the curtain, her soft snuffles filling the hut. Always the same in the monotony of years Thabo had been employed in the diamond mines. Lucky to have work. Lucky! Resentment twisted in her gut. His wages one-tenth those of a white miner: a few days with his family every nine months, a bare week at Christmas. No sick leave. The barrack blocks he was forced to live in, a cage for beasts. Overcrowded, Sipho's father said, glad when they sacked him for returning for his wife's funeral, there you will go mad in the end. Your whole thinking becomes warped, you grow like an animal, act like one. She stood dutifully, lifting her face for Thabo's kisses as he left, then watched her mother's hunched figure scurry to the curtain. No life. There was no life.

Olla stayed on the mattress all afternoon, lulled to a drowsy contentment by the musky smell of sweat that was Thabo's. Vaguely she was aware of Godfrey, Nkulie, whispering about the room but as long as she kept her eyes closed she could still sense Thabo's presence. Later, old Mdala came for his mealie meal, his long nails scraping as he scooped the stiff mixture from the tin. Even when his dog ran whimpering about the room, she did not stir. Nkulie would deal with it. Black rag over the window. Flat on the mats till it was over. Strange the way the dogs always sensed it long before it came.

But tonight the growl of the Hippos came almost immediately, the dog instantly silent as the ground trembled. 'Thabo,' she whispered, 'Thabo.' She sealed her mind against the random scud of buckshot ploughing the lifeless dust of the yard, the scream of rubber bullets against the galvanised walls. 'There is a park, so beautiful, painted like the pale fingers of the madam I worked for in Durban. A beach with sand as fine as silk. Orchards of dark green avocado. One day, Thabo, we will taste it all.' She slid her fingers into her wide nostrils to block the smell of burning rubber that suddenly invaded the room, clinging to the image until the noise receded enough for her to know that they were safe. Tonight.

———

Nkulie joined the Comrades, staying after school to be educated, politicised, as Sipho had called it. She helped run one of the support committees for the families of those who were detained, tortured, under the State of Emergency. Joined the students boycotting the schools. Stoned the big houses and shops of the town councillors levying crippling rents. Carried paper banners hastily worded in thick felt-tip. 'Self-elected collaborators of the system,' the slogans read. 'You are the bricks in the wall of Apartheid.' The look-out scouts posted on every corner gave piercing whistles at the first sign of an approaching Casspir or police Hippo. Though Olla would find out soon enough, she swore Godfrey to silence for the mornings she began missing school. Hunkering over the rush mat where she sat, he rocked quickly back and forwards.

'Will they let me join too?'

'When you're older.'

'How old?'

'Twelve.'

'But that's three years away!'

Nkulie smiled. 'It will still be a children's war. It will always be a children's war. I'll teach you some songs while you're waiting.' She leapt up, grabbing Godfrey's arm, raising it in a fist over his head, began doing the 'toi-toi', the running march, danced to the freedom songs. 'Listen!'

'Liberation will be gained

when our children have been trained.

Don't you lose hope,

there's work to be done.

War together, children for

the victory to be won.

War together child —'

'Enough!' Olla stood stony-faced in the open doorway. 'So this is what you teach him while I tend to old Mdala! Godfrey, take the basin for water. And come straight back. It's getting late.'

The boy ran without a word, glad to be out of it.

'New. Where've you learnt it?'

Nkulie scuffed her canvas shoe against the concrete. 'Around.' She lifted thin shoulders in a shrug. 'Sipho, probably.'

'You'd best forget such songs. His father was with Mdala. He says the police wouldn't give him any information. He doesn't hold out much hope. You want to know what he said? He said to me, "Olla, my boy will either come back to me a piece of blubbering pulp, or I will never see him again. Which thing should I wish for, Olla?" You'll end up the same as Sipho. You'll break our hearts.'

'Poor Sipho.' Nkulie turned to hide it, staring through the window. The day was cooling, the sun trapped in the galvanised huts stacked like bullion along the street. In the distance, Godfrey's small frame disappeared round the corner towards the water pump.

'You must forget him. He was an agitator.'

'Agitator?' Nkulie swung around, hands on hips. 'Jesus, lord, you sound like one of them. Don't you know that's their word for anyone who protests? Who speaks out? Sipho was right when he said we have parents like sheep. Timid. Well, the children have anger enough for all of us!'

'Children! What sense have any of you? You're destroying your futures, your careers —'

'What careers? A black lawyer in this country has more in common with a black labourer than a white law student. Education for blacks?' Nkulie snorted. 'You want to know what Verwoerd said when he introduced inferior education for us? "It isn't wise to permit African children to gaze on pastures upon which they can never hope to graze." Bantu education, Bantustans, Bantu courts. Any time you hear the word "Bantu", you can be sure it means something bad for blacks!'

'Where are you learning —? Not at school —'

'Who has to teach me this? I'm living with it!'

'You've joined.' Olla spoke quietly, but the certainty in her voice cut through Nkulie's words.

'Yes. I've joined the Comrades.'

They stared at each other, eyes flickering for some sign of weakness. In the silence of those moments, the faint vibrations in the tinny walls, they became aware of the rumble of the Casspirs over the uneven surface of the streets, the distant shooting. Not even dark yet.

'Godfrey!' Olla's hands went to her face, her gaze petrified.

'I'll find him!' Nkulie was gone before Olla could scream at her to stop. Through the window she caught a glimpse of the ribbon threading her daughter's hair as she slunk around the side of the hut, heading for the rocky bank at the bottom of the yard. Olla scanned the street, her eyes taking in the rangy dog skulking into one of the yards opposite, its tail hidden between its legs as it slipped out of sight. Nothing moved.

'He knows to keep away. He knows. How often have I warned him. Don't go to look. They'll take you too. A good boy. Clever. He'll remember, hide somewhere until it's over. He will. I know he will. Drop it, Godfrey. Drop the basin and run. Run!' She shivered, hardly aware she'd spoken aloud. Still she held the black rag, delaying 'till the last moment, but as the sun speared the grey Hippo lurching into the rutted street, she reached finally to hang it, blotting out what little light the window shed. Startled, she heard a soft thump against the door, the quiet sigh breathing through its surface.

'Godfrey? Nkulie?' Cautiously she tip-toed to open it, surprised at its heavy spring inwards until Godfrey fell forward. His eyes rolled, the whites glistening as his face blanked into unconsciousness. She dragged him in quickly, terrified he'd be seen. Only when she had laid him on her mattress, lit the candle, did she discover where he was wounded. Birdshot in the right shoulder. In the back. She fought the tears, her jaw working angrily. How many times had she seen this among the children, the women? Always, always in the back. As they tried to run away. A low sound snarled from her throat. She could see the dull splinters embedded in the flesh. Open to the bone. But he'd live.

Dimly she was aware of the sounds outside. As long as the raiding didn't go on all night. Not the hospital. There, police would be waiting inside the casualty section, ready to grab whoever turned up. If you were shot, you were guilty. She'd take him to the church. The white priest, as good as a doctor. For now she had to keep him cool, herself busy, calm. She went to soak a rag in the leftover tea, swivelling in mid-step, the candle guttering as the door crashed inwards. So intent had she been, the sounds outside hadn't penetrated. Now a whole chorus pitched into the room along with the man who blundered in, filling the small space. His ugliness shocked her. She stared at the billowing ears, the nose which dwarfed his eyes, the hands like stout mallets, and could not think past what she saw. He kicked the door, slamming it shut. The thud of bullets, the shouts, retreated, hovered in the corrugated creases of the walls.

He'd been drinking, a beer bottle held to attention in one hand, a rifle trailing loosely from the other. Army? Paramilitary police? The green khaki told her nothing.

'Jou naam, munt!' He blinked rapidly, the long bottle pressed to his chin, drooping like a tusk. If she could keep him from Godfrey.

All that mattered. She answered his questions in Afrikaans, the steadiness of her voice surprising her as she fought the urge to look towards the curtain. She began to tremble as he moved about, his gaze wandering to the cheap cloth that hid her son.

'Your children? Where?' He swung the bottle towards the curtain, beer spurting in a thin stream.

'Not here.' Olla inched sideways to stand between him and Godfrey. Please, please, she thought.

'On the streets? Giving us trouble? Fucking little kaffirs. Little commie bastards.'

'No, no! Good children. Visiting their grandmother. The other side of town. My mother is old, sick,' she lied. 'They cook for her.'

'So your old man's in the mines.' He clacked his tongue against his teeth, a mockery of the Xhosa click, small lashless eyes roving her body. 'Missing it, are you? That filthy black dick rammed up you, making more little tsotsis to shit all over South Africa? As if twenty-two million baboons isn't enough. Fucking for you koelies ought to be declared illegal. A subversive activity.' His laugh rang against the iron walls. Olla stared at her feet, the submissive stance blacks took in the presence of a white. To look them in the eye was to antagonise, challenge, declare yourself their equal. Words. What were they? The trick was to let them slide over you, disappear. As long as Godfrey stayed unconscious, his breathing too shallow to be heard above the Boer's loud voice.

But she jumped as he reached suddenly, his hand delving into the vee of her frock. She strained backwards as he yanked the flimsy material to pull her closer. Her ears filled with a rush of sound like a zip being undone as the bodice ripped to her waist. He stared at her breasts, pushing her against the table.

'... soldiers. God's work I'm doing, don't you know that? Botha should give me a medal for saving him one more headache. I'll fuck you up so good you won't ever want another prick inside you this side of Hell.'

She stood rigid, her hands behind, gripping one of the table boards as he tore at her body. The pain radiated instantaneously, centring in her stomach, the blood pulsing furiously in her ears. She did not contemplate resisting. To live was the thing. Her life.

Godfrey's. Concentrate. Take him to the church. Tend to him until he was well again. Look, see him there in the yard, running with the other children. Teasing old Mdala's dog. Concentrate. Nkulie? Nonkululeko. Her full name the music of freedom. Daughter, you were right. Safer on the streets than in this room. This home. Trap. What was it you asked? Thabo, Thabo, is this a life? What you slave in the mines for? What we're segregated in the townships for, banished to the homelands for? This, this ... violation? Raped people, homes, tracts of land. Even our children raped of their childhood, their education. No life between them and us. No life. There are no trees for us, Thabo, no parks, no beaches, no orchards dripping with fruit. For us there is the industry of death, rocks and veldt dust, tin huts, tearsmoke and bullets. This is our prison.

When she came to, Olla was alone, conscious only of pain. She couldn't centre it, identify where it stemmed from. Or why. The candle was on the floor. Burning in a pool of wax. The door was closed. The distant sounds of raiding in other streets echoed in the walls, forced her to remember. Godfrey! She dragged herself from the boards, staggered forwards, lunging at the curtain as she fell. The frayed piece of twine that held it snapped and she scrabbled frantically to pull the cloth from her face.

Godfrey lay oblivious. Still breathing, the wound a congealed mess. Soon she could take him. She'd have to call Mdala, take his ancient, rusted barrow. Something oozed through his shirt and she cried out. But as she leaned forward, blood dripped from her own body, staining another part of his chest. Looking down she saw her left nipple hanging from a thread of flesh, the breast distended like an overblown balloon. She was still vomiting by the side of the mattress when Nkulie slid swiftly into the hut. The girl stared open-mouthed, eyes glittering as they swept her mother's tattered body, Godfrey's stillness.

'Jesus lord! Is he —?'

Olla shook her head, finally controlling her shudders. 'Wounded. The shoulder. I'm taking him to Father John.'

'Animals! What have they —?' Nkulie moved forward nervously, hands outstretched.

'Don't ask!'

'Let me — You're —' She knuckled her eyes, fighting the help-lessness.

Olla struggled to rise. 'Go! Go help the Comrades kill the bas-tards! Use stones, sticks, necklaces!' She winced as she pulled the shreds of the dress over her breasts. 'Go kill them all! With my blessing. Your father's blessing. You were right, daughter. There is no life.'

Nkulie felt it coming slowly, the fever, the hungry excitement Sipho's words stirred in her. She wanted to run now, be with the others in the thick of it before Olla lost her anger.

'How will you manage? You can't carry —'

'Mdala will help. Go.'

'Sure?' For one fleeting instant Nkulie saw how it would be in the streets, what the others had told her. She was afraid. She took a step forward, then hesitated. They had never been demonstrative with each other. Olla's puffed lips twisted in a grimace. 'I thought that's what you wanted.' The words were dull, flat, almost an accusation. Nkulie turned and fled, her mother's howl chasing her till she lost herself in the cover of the rubble-strewn bank. There she stayed until the choking breaths drowned in a tide of fury propelling her forwards. In the evening light the last shrapnel of sunlight lingered, smudges of blood in the sky. Pale stars flickered incessantly like bursts of gunfire.

She knew where to find them. In the tunnel under the crumbling dam, making Molotov cocktails to throw at the armoured wagons, soaking towels to protect themselves from the smoke grenades. She fought her way through the rocks towards the sounds, eyes sting-ing, nostrils quivering as she caught the vile suffocating whiff of teargas, the stench of burning tyres. Where the bank dipped sharply towards the dry river-bed, she lay and watched the street, startled suddenly by the chirp of a cricket close to her ear. Police were looting an Indian liquor store, passing crates to the soldiers in one of the Casspirs. Two other shops burning. Further up the street, a small crowd jeering, throwing stones. Suddenly police and soldiers, faces masked, poured from the side streets, shooting randomly. The crowd scattered, people dropping like puppets with their strings cut. Others were chased, caught, kicked, whipped with knobkerries, batons, forced towards the waiting, windowless Kombis. A woman's body exploded under the direct hit of a teargas canister.

From a shadowy laneway, two policemen hauled someone out. The camera he held fell to the ground, one of the policemen smashing it underfoot, the other whipping viciously at the man's head. Suddenly he broke free, running across the street towards the bank where she lay, his white face a bizarre negative of her own terror. The policemen gave chase, collecting others as they ran.

Nkulie panicked. He would lead them right to her. Jumping up, she turned, careering down the rocky slope as the shouts behind her thickened. Away from the dam, she thought, the wall of bladed wire that twisted in a wide sweep on the town's perimeters, hemming them in. Across the river bed towards the graveyard, into the mock grave the priest had dug. Let me make it. Is there a God for blacks? She heard the sound of the quirt before it struck, the braided plait of rhinoceros hide whining past her ear to whip her shoulders. Her knees buckled at the sudden shock of pain and she keeled over, curling in a tight stiff shell against the kicks, the blows that would come. Fear clawed at her insides and she squeezed instinctively on the muscles in her groin, afraid she would wet herself.

'Look, a houtkop, a dirty black football. You think if we kick it, it'll roll to the bottom of the bank?'

'What if it bursts? We'd have nothing to play with.'

Nkulie curled tighter, eyes closed, their laughter rasping in her ears, refusing to think beyond the next moment, what they might do. Each moment is a separate life. Tick, tick, tick. That's what it is, how you get through it, Sipho said.

'She could use a haircut. Hey, Frieky, got your knife?'

A hand grasped a bunch of her hair and the pain made her leap up, stumble with them as they dragged her down the slope. There were three of them, two middle-aged, grey crew cuts, one blond, little more than her own age.

'Here's a nice clean puddle. You have a good wash, you black scum.' The older men began laughing again as she crouched, scooping the rancid slime, rubbing it with trembling fingers on her

face. The younger policeman stood apart, narrow shoulders twitching, eyes distant.

'Now that lice-ridden frizzball. Frieky, give Piet the knife. Come on, man, your first day in action, time you had a little fun, cured that queasy stomach of yours.'

Nkulie gazed numbly at the young policeman holding the knife, aware of his unease, his distaste. She saw it in his eyes: what he had learned in his mother's arms, at his father's knee, in the schools, from the pulpit. The unequal struggle between that and his sudden recognition of her, the shock of glimpsing the myth that made racism. He had a thin, sensitive face, not unlike Sipho's. Except he was white. True blue Afrikaner white. He would do what they wanted in the end, rather than become the butt of their jokes, the object of their hatred.

'What's the matter? You like black bitches? Jesus, maan, whose side are you on?'

The taunt spurred him to action. She shrank as his hands leapt at her hair, hacking it jaggedly. She smelt the fear in him, the revulsion that matched her own. Angered by what he had sensed, much rougher than he need have been, wanting to deny it, prove himself. She closed her eyes against the self-loathing in his, seeing suddenly that he was the most dangerous of the three.

'Better, hey? What about a little jewellry to go with the new hairstyle? A nice necklace, maybe?'

She heard her own scream, a high-pitched, stricken sound as the fragile thread of control snapped, the single moments crowding before her into hours of burning flesh. Once she had seen it: an informer, the tyre doused in petrol set alight about his neck, body bound and writhing, the screams endless until the mind snapped, the stink of charred skin in her nostrils for weeks. She'd rather die. Quickly, quickly.

'Stop screaming, you bitch! We're going to burn you black as coal.'

There was a blinding flash as something struck the side of her head and she welcomed the dizziness, hoping she would pass out.

'... won't be long. If she moves, give it to her in the mouth.'

She opened her eyes, registering the two men clambering up the

slope, the younger one standing with the rifle trained on her. She breathed deeply, trying to control the tremors. Her only chance. She had maybe a few minutes before they came back. To persuade him. To woo him.

'Stinking white pig,' she said, and spat.

He stiffened, his grip on the rifle tightening.

'War, together, children, war together children,' she sang softly. 'See in my eyes, the stink of victory.' She smiled, the fear leaving her, the skin all over her body tingling pleasantly. As though Sipho were stroking her. 'There is no safe place for you,' she said, rocking sensuously, watching him through half-closed eyes. 'Not on the streets, not in your home. One night when you are fucking your white girl, wrapped in your white sheets, you will remember shaving the head of a black girl who fucks a black boy. A black boy who looks like you.'

'Shut up!' he snapped, eyes jerking towards the empty slope.

'Sipho will come for you. A thousand Siphos. A thousand girls like me, carrying garlands of burning tyres to place about your neck.'

'Shut up or I'll blow your head off!' He pushed the cold barrel against her mouth. She pressed her lips to it, her eyes drowsy, unfocused.

'Our Father,' she began, the words low, husky, 'which art in South Africa, justice be Thy name, Thy liberation come —'

'— Shut up you black bitch!'

'Thy salvation be done not as it is in Namibia, but as it is in Lusaka, give us this day our daily weapons, our military training and forgive us our past timidity as we strive against our white oppressors and lead us not to Apartheid but deliver us from its evil, for Thine is the non-racial kingdom, the power and the victory —'

'Fokker! Swartgat! Jou ma se poes!' He rammed the barrel into her mouth as she stared up at him, eyes shining. Just before he pulled the trigger, she caught a glimpse of it, the fear that she had stoked, the fear that drove the hatred wreathing from his eyes like tearsmoke to blind her, choke her, open her skin in suppurating wounds as her lungs exploded, her vision shattered into a thousand pinheads of light.